curse of the
Bone pirates

nui island
ECO-LOGICAL ADVENTURES

B.T. HOPE

Published by Nui Media & Entertainment
P.O. Box 364
Santa Monica, CA 90406

For ordering information or special discounts for bulk purchases, please contact Greenleaf Book Group LLC at: 4425 South Mo Pac Expwy., Suite 600 Austin, TX 78735, (512) 891-6100.

Illustrations and cover design by Tina DiCicco
Design and composition by Greenleaf Book Group LLC

Publisher's Cataloging-In-Publication Data
(Prepared by The Donohue Group, Inc.)

Hope, B. T.
 The curse of the Bone Pirates : Nui Island eco-logical adventures / B.T. Hope. -- 1st ed.

 p. : ill. ; cm.

 Summary: Big B. is dragged from his comfortable life and friends in Chicago by his grandfather's mysterious affliction and he is sure he is going to have the worst summer ever. But soon after arriving in the tropical paradise of Nui Island, he is caught in a web of danger and intrigue. To save the island and restore his grandfather's soul he has to break the curse of the Bone Pirates.
 ISBN: 978-0-9817388-0-2

 1. Pirates--Juvenile fiction. 2. Imaginary places--Juvenile fiction. 3. Island ecology--Juvenile fiction. 4. Adventure and adventurers--Juvenile fiction. 5. Pirates--Fiction. 6. Adventure and adventurers--Fiction. I. Title.

PZ7.H67 C8 2008
[Fic]   2008934120

Printed in the United States of America on acid-free paper

Part of the Tree Neutral™ program that offsets the number of trees consumed in printing this book by taking proactive steps such as planting trees in direct proportion to the number of trees used. www.treeneutral.com

TreeNeutral

10 09 08   10 9 8 7 6 5 4 3 2 1

First Edition

Contents

Prologue

Cursed!

Raindrops fell, but Professor Prune didn't even notice. He was wrist deep in bones. And they were human bones—skulls, fibulas, scapulas, and all the other bones that make up the human skeleton. He had tied a bandana over his nose and mouth to protect him from the foul odor, but his eyes still watered behind his half-inch-thick glasses. Despite the overwhelming evidence of death, the Professor was extremely excited. "Fascinating . . . fascinating," he muttered to himself as he examined one bone after another, laying them out in the shape of a body. "Which one could he be?"

Hundreds of bones and clamshells were scattered across a volcanic plateau, high on an island in the middle of the Pacific Ocean. The

Professor's research had proven fruitful, and the mere thrill of finding the four-hundred-year-old bones would have been uncontainable, if not for his questions that were still unanswered. *Why had the bones recently become exposed? Did anyone else know they were here? Why were there clamshells at this elevation? Which skull belonged to Ratbeard?* He stopped and took a better look at his surroundings.

Raising his head to wipe the sweat from his brow, and then the fog from his glasses, the Professor realized that he had lost track of time. And he was getting wet. The usual summer evening rainfall that had begun should have told him that it was past eight o'clock. Raindrops plopped all around him. The sky was growing a much darker grey and thunder rumbled very close by. "I've got to find him!" he exclaimed, though no one around him was alive to hear.

The Professor made his way upward, through spirals of steam generated by the volcanic springs. The steam rose like ghosts, curling up through the scraggly bushes, then disappeared into the falling rain. He suspected that there were more bones in the bushes. As he parted the branches, he noticed that the leaves were turning brown along the edges and many had fallen off. And the tall grasses that normally surrounded the springs were limp and dying. He stood, looked around, puzzled. "What's going on here?"

The Professor climbed up to examine one cluster of bushes, running his hands down their woody stems. He couldn't help noticing that the foul odor seemed to be stronger at this higher elevation compared to where he'd been searching further down the hill.

As he explored the bushes, he found more of the same shells that were strewn across the plateau. They seemed old but still intact.

"Could it be? Did *he* put these here?" he asked aloud to himself while squinting to get a better view.

It was getting darker and harder to see, so he reached into his pack for his flashlight. He stopped suddenly. Through the branches of the bushes, he glimpsed light. A phosphorescent glow seemed to twinkle in the spring that fed the stream flowing down the mountain. The spring had formed a deep, dark pool.

"What on earth?" Professor Prune pushed the branches aside, following the light. He stopped and blinked his eyes. Small bones, like a bird's, floated among large rocks in the pool. He knew immediately that they weren't human bones and not who he was looking for.

Just as he pulled his flashlight out of his pack to examine the bones more closely, the sky flashed a blinding white. Electricity filled the air as a zigzag of lighting struck the bones, turning them, and the pool, an eerie electric blue. As he leapt back, a deep boom rattled the Professor's own bones. His foot landed against a round rock that rolled to the side, taking the Professor's foot with it. The Professor lurched forward and reached out for a branch to steady himself, but the branch, weak and brittle, snapped and the Professor went sprawling.

He landed in a pile of bones and clamshells that crushed beneath the force of his fall. A fine green dust rose from the shells, seeming to emanate from their broken contours. The Professor lay still for a moment, then slowly and carefully rolled over onto his back, listening to the bones and shells crunch under his weight. He took a deep breath, sat up, and then slowly rose to a standing position. He brushed his hands over his clothing, surveying the damage. Skinned knees, torn pants, a few cuts, and a layer of green dust, which was quickly turning into a sticky goo in the rain. Nothing too serious. He turned his attention back to the blue bones, but they were gone, and a strange creature now sat on a rock that was half-submerged in the pool. The creature seemed to smolder—even sizzle—in the raindrops. *Did it just move? How could it after a hundred million volts of electricity?* he wondered.

The Professor sneezed. He felt a little dizzy. He suddenly forgot why he was there. Lying beside him in the green dust was a small metal cylinder capped with a skull, with blue stones—surely glass—set in the eye sockets. He brushed off the dust and polished it with his sleeve. "Wonderful," he said. "Brett will love this." He fished a padded envelope out of his backpack and wrote his grandson's name and address on it, to be sure he wouldn't forget to mail it.

The Professor wished he could see his grandson's smiles of curiosity when Brett opened the many gifts he had sent him. He wondered if his grandson had that same yearning for discovery, for adventure, that had led the Professor on journeys around the world. But the Professor couldn't deal with that question; he suddenly felt very ill and confused. A tickling sensation ran over his forehead and down his cheeks. And when had it turned so dark? He tried to brush away whatever was tickling his face and searched his clothes with his flashlight for whatever might have been crawling on him.

Finding nothing, he directed the light to the ground, where he spotted a black feather tumbling gently around his feet in the gusty wind. He picked it up and felt a small electrical charge between his fingers. He looked around, growing more and more confused, then began to walk.

As he rummaged in his pack for a sample bag, his footsteps began to falter until he stopped moving altogether. He stood in the dark, staring at the ground. Absentmindedly, he raised his arm to scratch his cheek. "Now what was . . . screm . . . do . . . kafle?" The Professor slowly looked around, confused by his surroundings. "Where . . . manch . . . blarn?" He looked blankly at his pack, holding it loosely in one hand, then let it drag on the ground.

He began wandering down the side of the mountain, occasionally stumbling and catching himself on branches and boulders. The farther he descended, the more erratic his steps became. Staggering, he began to slip in the loose soil and then he began to slide helplessly down a rocky ledge—and then over it. He flailed his arms in a half-hearted attempt to catch himself, but it was useless.

Professor Prune had fallen into the mouth of a cave. As he rolled down the incline, his small pickax, brushes, and shovel tumbled from his pack. He came to rest in a pile of rubble, moaning as he slipped into unconsciousness. But for one brief moment he was aware of his surroundings and in that moment he shouted one word.

"Pirates!"

Chapter 1
5,700 miles from home

Big B's flaming-red hair flattened against the window as he peered out at the endless blue ocean 35,000 feet below him. From his airplane seat, he could see only water, reaching out to the horizon in all directions. He had already read the book he brought, flipped through two airline magazines, and listened to his entire collection of Bent Lizard, his new favorite band, three times. Now the real boredom was kicking in. To pass time, Big B started running through some important calculations in his head. *If we're traveling at about five hundred miles per hour, and we've been over the ocean for nearly three hours, then we're about fifteen hundred miles from Hawaii, which is forty-two hundred miles from Chicago. So . . . fifty-seven hundred miles from home. Five thousand . . .*

Big B liked numbers. They always made sense even if the rest of the world didn't. His mom nudged him, so he reluctantly pulled out his earphones and turned to her.

"Brett, did you know that right now we're the farthest away from a continent you can get on the planet? There is ocean for thousands of miles around us."

"Yeah, Mom, I sort of noticed." Big B turned back to the window. He realized his mom was trying to start a conversation, but he wasn't interested in talking. And he wasn't thrilled about the thousands of miles of ocean under him, either.

I bet we've flown over thousands of sharks, he thought, pulling up his sleeve to look at the shark his best friend, Jack, had drawn with a blue permanent marker on his arm. They had met in Big B's tree house only an hour before he had had to leave for the airport. While Jack finished Big B's tattoo, they had talked about all of the cool things he was going to miss in the last few days of school—especially a field trip to the aquarium and the school carnival. He never thought he would miss school so much. Jack had tried to make him feel better. "You've been to the aquarium before, and the carnival is lame." But Jack hadn't been able to look Big B in the eye when he had said it—he knew what Big B was going to miss.

Big B's hero, skater Jeremy Cliff, was coming to the carnival this year for a skateboarding demonstration. Jeremy was amazing: He had placed second in the X Games all because of his signature trick, the daring "Cliff-hanger." A 720 with so much air it defied gravity. Big B's attempt at that trick was what got him into major trouble the day before he and his mom left Chicago.

His friends dared him to do crazy stuff all the time, and he would eagerly do it. Unfortunately, things usually ended up with something getting broken (once his arm), his friends scattering, and him getting grounded. So when his friends dared him to try the Cliff-hanger, he thought that maybe he shouldn't. They were hanging out at the mall, practicing tricks on the great concrete ramp that ran next to the stairs leading to the lower level. He knew it wasn't likely that he'd pull the move off, but they just kept bugging him about it, and try as he might, he couldn't resist. *What's the worst that can happen?* he thought. Unfortunately, he found out the answer to that question.

The jump, like many before, did not go as planned. When he hit the ground, far short of his intended landing, only his helmet and pads saved him from personal wreckage. But his board had caught some serious air! So much air that he could watch the action from where his head lay on the concrete. The fire-painted board flew as if in slow motion—and then smacked against a metal light pole, ringing it like a bell. Big B thought that was the end of the show, but no . . . The board rocketed off the pole, and struck dead center in the gigantic front window of Rocco's Pizza.

Big B lifted his head up in time to see the manager, tossing a big round piece of dough in the air like a Frisbee, jump back, drop the dough, and then cover his head with his arms as a giant spiderweb of cracks spread across the huge pane of glass. For what seemed like hours, silence engulfed Big B as everyone stared at the window. Just as Big B thought the damage was complete, the entire window crumbled into a million little pieces, falling to the ground, spilling out like diamonds in every direction.

Big B sat on the stairs and put his head in his hands. His friends—even Jack—had suddenly disappeared. "You stay right there," Rocco yelled as he dialed mall security. When security showed up, they called Big B's mom.

Big B's mom had gotten calls like this before, so he had a good idea what her reaction would be. But this time, for some reason, she was calmer. Big B had done some pretty crazy things, but this was the first time she had ever picked him up at a security office. The principal's office was one thing, but the people here wore uniforms, talked on walkie-talkies, and carried police batons. Yet even though she looked as though she had been crying, she didn't yell at him. That freaked him out, but he pretended not to care. Instead, she listened to the security officer, glared at Big B, and then led him to the car with a firm grip on his arm. On the way home, she said only one thing: "When you get home I want you to pack. You and I are going to live with Grandpa for a while."

He had tried to ask her some questions, but she clearly was not in any mood to answer, so he gave up.

The next morning was frantic as they got ready to leave, but he eventually pinned his mom down. "Mom, what's going on? Why are we leaving like this? I'm going to miss the school carnival!"

"After the stunt you pulled yesterday, I wouldn't have let you go anyway, Brett."

"But it was my friends' idea!" His voice cracked into a high pitch.

"That's exactly the problem. Your need to impress and entertain your friends is going to end up with you in juvenile detention—or worse. But that's not the only reason why we're going," she paused. Her eyes glistened "I got a call yesterday about Grandpa. He needs us and we're going, end of discussion."

Big B fought back his own tears. *It wasn't fair. It was his friends' idea!*

"What about Dad?"

"Your father is too busy with work. He'll visit us if he can arrange a layover on his way back from China."

Big B's dad was the kind of businessman who invested money in new companies, called a venture capitalist. He was always traveling to faraway places. Big B thought that was cool. He liked to tell his friends that his dad was an *ad*venture capitalist. But Dad's cool job also meant he was never home to see Big B play football, help with his homework, or just be around.

Big B thought about his dad as he stared out the window again. Would his dad even be able to find them? His grandpa lived on some island-no-has-ever-heard-of in the middle of the South Pacific. He had a sudden horrible realization: The island might not have cable or cell phone coverage. How was he going to watch his favorite MMA fighters on TV? How was he going to call or text his friends? His life was about to end forever. That's exactly what he would text Jack—if he could . . . *Nd 4evr.*

"How long before that shark washes off?" His mom interrupted his depressing thoughts.

"I don't know. I hope it never goes away."

"By the time it's gone, I bet you'll be hanging out with new friends, enjoying the island life," she assured him.

"Yeah, whatever," he shrugged sullenly and turned his face back against the window. But she did look worried. "What do you think is wrong with Grandpa?"

"I don't know, honey. The caretaker of his land who called me said Grandpa's been acting very strange lately, confused, saying bizarre things. He thinks maybe Grandpa had a stroke . . . or worse." Her voice wavered as she looked away.

Big B hadn't seen his grandpa since he was too small to remember. He did know that he was a professor at the island university, and his mom had said he was super smart. Grandpa had never visited them in Chicago, but after spending eleven hours on planes, Big B could understand why. Instead, Grandpa sent weird holiday and birthday gifts, like a feather from some mysterious tropical bird, a native islander mask, or an old piece of pottery. Big B kept all the funky gifts in a wrinkled old leather bag that had held the mask. The bag was in his suitcase.

The day before they left Chicago, the mailman had delivered another gift from his grandpa—a cool pendant on a leather string. It was a silver-colored cylinder about as big around as his index finger and so polished and shiny it reflected like a mirror. When he held the cylinder up to his face, his reflection was warped into the craziest-looking face; Jack's looked even funnier. But the cylinder's cap was the coolest part. It was a skull, with eyes set with blue stones, bright blue like his own eyes. He wondered if they might even be real sapphires. It looked as though it had come from some ancient burial ground, but it smelled a bit fishy, like an old seashell.

That gift was too cool for the bag, so Big B wore it around his neck. Other kids always asked him about the things his grandpa sent him, and he liked to brag about how it was a piece of ancient treasure—probably pirate treasure—to guard. Maybe when he got to the island he could become a pirate. Big B, the flame-haired pirate. Yeah, a pirate who's always getting busted by his mom!

Just as he was about to ask how soon they would be going home, the small plane slowed a little, banked hard to the left, and then began to descend. His stomach dropped—as if he were on a roller coaster—and he grabbed the armrests, gripping them tightly. Big B pressed his face to the glass to see where they were headed. The sea had changed color, from a deep blue to an electric silver and bright turquoise that reminded him of the light that danced on the bottom of swimming pools in summertime.

Far below, a small, mountainous island broke up the flat expanse of ocean. Big B struggled to see it better, but as the plane continued to turn, the island passed out of view. He quickly unfastened his seatbelt and stood to look out another window, but his mom grabbed his arm and pulled him down.

"Sit down, Brett! We're getting ready to land."

The plane turned hard again, and the engines rumbled loudly. The flaps on the back edge of the plane's wing rotated down, and the plane slowed. As they descended, the island came back into view. The first thing Big B noticed was all the green—green mountainsides, green forests, green lawns. He could almost smell it, fresh, alive. A single city, buildings shining white and standing tall, interrupted the emerald landscape. Houses spread out and up from the city, dotting the hillsides. From the mountain cliffs, waterfalls sparkled and threw glowing rainbow arcs of red, orange, yellow, green, blue, indigo, and violet over the village below. Craggy clusters of black rock and white beaches separated the city from the sea.

Directly below the plane, the pulsing sea seemed to be rushing up toward them. Waves crashed into coral reefs just visible in the clear water. Among the curling waves, Big B could see a tiny orange boat. A wave crashed on top of it, startling Big B, but the boat popped up again. As the next wave loomed, the boat spun around. Big B realized it was a surfboard. The wave caught up to the board and the surfer stroked down the face. But the wave tumbled over and the surfer was gone. Before Big B could groan "wipeout," however, the orange-haired surfer popped out of the tube.

"Wow!"

It was the coolest thing he had ever seen—until a dolphin leapt out of the wave right next to the guy.

"No way!"

He tried to look back at them as they shrank away in the distance. Was the orange dude waving? The plane suddenly seemed so close to the water that Big B felt as if *he* was surfing. He started to wonder where the runway was. He gripped the armrests again, bracing for disaster. But the water turned into sand and sand became cement. Colors whizzed by, and the island felt brighter and more alive than any place he'd ever seen before.

With a thump, the plane touched down.

The pilot came over the loudspeaker, "Thanks for flying with us, folks. And welcome to Nui Island."

Big B couldn't help but smile.

Chapter 2
SÁM

the plane slowed on the runway. Big B strained against his seatbelt to tie his black wrestling shoes—his favorite shoes. Wrestling was the hardest sport he played, the one that made his body ache after practice. His shoes reminded him of all the "no pain, no gain" pep talks from his coach, who used it to push him to try harder, to go further. He felt tough when he was wearing these shoes, like he could handle any situation, could solve any problem.

The plane taxied toward the gate—the only gate—of the Nui Island Airport. Once it finally came to a stop, a tan guy in shorts connected a set of wobbly metal steps to the doorway, bridging the passengers to the asphalt below.

Big B and his mom strapped on their backpacks and headed down the steps. He went for two and then three steps at a time, followed by a mid-air 360° spin and a perfect landing at the bottom. "Sick!"

He looked up at his mother, who was mouthing something, but he couldn't hear her. Bent Lizard pulsed in his ears as his other senses awakened from the long flight. A swift breeze ruffled his hair, and the bright sunshine warmed his face. The air was thick with moisture, as though a fresh rain had just passed. Reflecting the sun's rays, his necklace sent spots of light dancing across his chest and face. He looked down at the gift from Grandpa and tucked it under his shirt. The pendant felt unusually cool against his skin.

Big B took a deep breath. He noticed this place had a smell that was new and very different from home. It was hard to describe. It smelled clean, like his soap, mixed with sea salt and warm, ripe fruit. He took another deep breath, turned off his iPod, and then turned to his mom.

"So now what? Where's Grandpa's house?"

"They said Sam would meet us at the airport. So I guess we need to find someone who looks like a Sam."

Big B followed his mom into the airport's terminal. Actually, it didn't look much like a terminal; it was just a big room with folding chairs and potted palms. He scanned the room for Sam. Was it the big dude covered in tattoos? Or maybe the tall, thin guy with shaggy hair and a beach hat? The bald guy with glasses? Then he recognized his last name written in purple marker on a yellow piece of paper: WELCOME HARRINGTONS. Big B looked up at the guy holding the sign—only to realize it was not a guy at all, it was a girl.

The sign holder seemed to be about his age. She was small, almost a head shorter than Big B, yet she looked strong and muscular. She peered at him with large, greenish eyes framed by long, thick hair dyed a deep purple. Her grape-toned hair was accented by a lavender streak woven into a long braid and a pink tropical flower tucked behind her ear.

Purple hair? He thought. *I like red better.*

He must have been staring, because the girl suddenly put one hand on her hip and raised an eyebrow. "Looking for something, *Gallo?*" she said with a slight accent.

Caught off guard by her feisty attitude, Big B was about to stammer a response until he noticed her necklace. It was gold with an oval stone in the center that glowed pearly white against her tan skin. But what had distracted him was that the stone seemed to be changing color, turning a deeper and deeper red as Sam continued to regard him as though he were some kind of insect. Big B pulled his gaze away from the necklace and stepped forward to introduce himself, but his cell phone beeped in his pocket, letting him know that he had a text message. He used the distraction to save him from an awkward moment. He turned away and flipped his phone open to read the message. Instead of a text, a surreal image appeared on the screen. It was warped, like a smeared paint-ing with oddly placed letters and squiggles. It looked like one of those paintings that made no sense, the ones his mom called "Modernist."

"Stupid spam," Big B mumbled.

"What?"

"Uh, we're, uh, looking for some guy named Sam."

"I'm Sam, you silly *gallo rojo!*" she smirked. She draped necklaces of sweet-smelling flowers around Big B's and his mom's necks. "Welcome to Nui Island," she said, smiling purposely at Big B's mom. "*Bienvenido.*" She winked at Big B.

"Thank you, Sam," replied his mom, nudging him.

"Yeah," scoffed Big B, "thanks *mucho.*" Big B didn't know what Sam had called him—what a guy-o ro-ho was—but it sounded like she was speaking Spanish, and *mucho* was one of the few Spanish words he knew. Sam's green eyes narrowed; she had obviously caught the mockery in Big B's tone. His mom turned and glared at him.

Finally, Sam broke the silence, again addressing his mom. "Come on. Let's get your luggage. My dad's waiting out front in the Cruiser." Outside, a cream-colored, safari-style truck waited at the curb. It was like no truck Big B had ever seen, one suited for the savannahs of Africa. Sam's dad literally jumped out. He grabbed their luggage and piled it up in the back of the truck.

"Welcome, my friends! I'm Armando Flores, Professor Prune's groundskeeper and most loyal friend," he said, with an ear-to-ear smile and a wink at Sam. Sam rolled her eyes in response, but grinned back.

"Climb aboard, everyone!" Armando called out as he hauled himself into the driver's seat. Big B and his mom climbed into the open back seat, glad that there was nothing on the truck to obscure any of their dazzling view.

Armando started the Cruiser's rumbling engine after the second try and they followed the road out of the airport up into the emerald green hills. Taking in the scenery, Big B was still amazed by the colors and smells of Nui Island. The bright, white sands and sparkling blue ocean, the salty fresh air, the smell of baked banana bread . . . *Wait . . . banana bread?*

"Hey, this island smells like banana bread!" he shouted to Armando.

"Actually, it's the Cruiser," Armando replied over his shoulder. "This week it's fueled by banana peels and other banana parts. We just harvested a lot of bananas. And sometimes sugar cane. Or algae, but that makes it smell like the ocean."

"What? No way! You're just kidding me, right?"

"No, really. You can make ethanol out of all kinds of plants," Armando yelled back. "And ethanol replaces the gasoline we used to use in the engine."

"A banana-burning truck? Who came up with that wacky idea?"

"Your grandpa did!" Sam whipped around in her seat with a look of pride. "He's a genius."

"More like crazy," laughed Big B. Suddenly, everyone was silent. Big B realized his embarrassing mistake too late. He probably shouldn't have used the word *crazy*, with his grandfather behaving strangely.

With no one talking, Big B could hear sounds above the rumble of the banana truck's engine that he hadn't noticed before. Birds screeched, insects buzzed, and the roar of hidden waterfalls could be heard through the thick ferns and bushes alongside the road. After what felt like forever, Armando broke the uneasy silence.

"We are here, my friends!" he proclaimed, as they pulled up to a bamboo gate flanked by stone pillars. Through the gate Big B could see a simple wooden bridge spanning a small gully. To the right, the hillside rose steeply, setting the stage for a beautiful waterfall. The waterfall splashed down into the gully, casting a fine, cooling mist into the air and creating a small stream that rambled under the bridge. Everywhere, trees and vines grew in dense abundance.

Everything about the scene was perfect, but Big B felt a chill run up his spine. Maybe it was the damp spray or the deep shadows cast by the palms and dense undergrowth. There were so many places for creatures to hide. Big B had never been in a tropical forest before, and he felt uncertain.

"Sam, I like your new addition," Armando said, looking up at the driftwood sign hanging overhead, with unfamiliar words burned into it.

Big B struggled to read the Spanish words. "*Vista . . . de los . . . Espíritus.* What does that mean?"

Sam turned to answer, and Big B noticed that her amulet was now glowing blue, "It's Spanish for what people here in the Pacific call *Nanaoka'uhane.*"

"And to us who only understand English?" Big B retorted, irritated by how unfamiliar everything was and slightly confused by the amulet's change of color.

"View of the spirits," Sam translated, almost whispering.

Big B looked back up at the sign, around which mist swirled in a breeze generated by the falling water. He shivered, even though it wasn't cold. The metal of his pendant felt like ice against his skin, and the hairs on the back of his neck rose. Just then, a dirty, bedraggled seagull landed on the hood of the car. It stared at them through the windshield.

Big B shifted in his seat and looked around uneasily. He had the strange sense that the seagull was watching him. It cocked its head one way and then the other but kept its beady eyes trained on him. It reminded him of the Johnson's cat back in Chicago. Every morning when he had delivered the Johnson's paper, their cat had stalked him, hiding in the dark hedges. He could hear it rustling, but he had never known quite where it was—until, of course, it leapt out at him, back arched, growling and hissing. He had fallen off his bike because of that cat. He had known it was always there watching . . . waiting.

"I call this place heaven," Armando said, happily. "It's a magical place. See, even the animals are stopping by to welcome you."

The seagull took off from the hood of the car but suddenly reversed directions and dove toward Big B in the open backseat. Big B's head jerked up as the seagull screeched, its long, pointed beak gaping.

In that fraction of a second Big B glimpsed a sharp beak, black feathers, and startling blue eyes coming straight for him. He ducked for cover but the horrible bird hovered above him. It screeched, and something wet hit his head. The bird flew off.

Chapter 3
felcome

Some *welcome!* Big B thought, as the lump of fear in his throat slowly subsided.

"I think it's gone," said Armando, a little breathless. "I've never seen a seagull behave like that before. Maybe it has a nest nearby that it's protecting . . . but most of them nest out on the cliffs."

Sam turned around in her seat, looking frightened. Suddenly she broke into hysterics and pointed. "It pooped on your head, Gallo Rojo! Ha-ha-ha!" Tears came to her eyes as she laughed harder. Big B reached his hand up to wipe the sappy goop from his hair. "Oh, that is so totally nasty!" Armando shot his daughter a stern look. "Oh!" she gasped, catching her breath while glancing at her father. "Oh, yeah, um, sorry, are you okay?" Stifling her laughter, she kept on saying "Sorry, sorry" in a not very convincing way. Then, "Here, use this." She handed him a tissue from the glove box.

"That bird was deranged!" Big B was shaken, and he didn't realize right away that he'd put his foot in his mouth again. "I mean . . . uh . . . sick. Maybe it's sick."

"Could be. Hmm. Well, let's get you folks to the house to see the Professor."

Armando hopped out of the Cruiser and opened the gate. The drive to the house was short but stunning—deep greens, giant tropical blooms, a waterfall, and brightly colored birds swooping overhead. Big B tried to control his instinct to duck again and again.

Armando swung the Cruiser around the drive and pulled up in front of the house. The house was like none Big B had ever seen. It looked a lot like a grand hut that a tribe of rain forest Indians would live in, but it had the modern feel of the science museum he used to visit back home. Bamboo and polished palm tree trunks framed the sides of the building into large squares and triangles, and open windows filled much of the exterior space. Rough black rocks and flowering vines decorated the spaces between all the windows. The roof was shiny like glass, but black. A dome that could have come from the Middle East rose up from the right side of the home. A long, covered wooden veranda ran along the front of the building. Potted plants and flowers hung from its roof. Birds flitted about, and even flew in and out of the open windows.

Two people stood on the veranda, an old man and a woman who looked a lot like Sam, only without the purple hair. The Cruiser came to a stop. Big B jumped out and pulled his backpack from the pile of luggage in the back. His mom immediately went to greet his grandfather.

"Hi, Dad!"

"Felcome, felcome," Professor Prune muttered as he hugged one of the pillars on the porch, mistaking it for Big B's mom.

"Uh, over here, Dad." She waved meekly. Confused, the Professor stared at the post for a moment, then tottered over to happily embrace his daughter.

Big B hung back, giving them a moment together. He felt a little uncertain about how to greet his grandfather. He didn't really know him, not to mention that he'd just hugged a post. His grandfather solved the dilemma by releasing his daughter and pulling his grandson into a bear hug. Big B was relieved that he didn't have to make the first move, but then his grandfather spoke.

"Felcome, by moy, doo gristahey toast less burritos!"

"Um . . . I'm sorry . . . What?" Big B asked, pulling away to look at his grandfather.

"He said, 'Welcome to Vista de los Espíritus,'" translated Sam, kindly patting the Professor on the shoulder.

"Oh, okay. Thanks, Grandpa. Your house is really cool." Big B spoke extra loud, hoping his Grandpa would understand him.

"He may be a little confused, Gallo, but he's not deaf," Sam said, looking smug.

"Geez! Bite my head off, Purple People-Eater." Big B turned red and looked away. "Sorry, Grandpa." His grandfather patted his arm, letting Big B know he had taken no offense.

"It's great to see you, Dad," assured his mom while exchanging worried glances with Big B. "We're excited to be staying with you. It's been a long time."

Big B studied his Grandpa while his mom talked and Sam translated the Professor's responses. *Grandpa Prune.* Big B couldn't believe his mom's last name used to be Prune! He couldn't decide if he should cringe in embarrassment or laugh his head off. His grandfather actually looked like a prune. His skin was brownish-purplish from years in the sun and creased by deep wrinkles. Topping off his face were half-inch-thick round glasses and a heavy white moustache that looked like his

BMX bike's handlebars, but upside down. The Professor was about as tall as Big B, if you counted the safari hat he was wearing.

Not only was the Professor's speech jumbled, but his clothes were also just as mixed up. The buttons on his island print shirt were misaligned, making him look off balance. His socks didn't match, and Big B thought perhaps his shorts were on backwards.

The woman standing with Big B's grandfather was Sam's mom. Armando introduced her: "Brett, Angela, this is my wife, Rosa."

Big B's mom hastily interrupted the introductions. "He likes to be called Big B now. It's a long story. Right, Brett?" She laughed and added, "He's still Brett to me!"

"Hola, welcome . . . Big B, . . . Angela," said Rosa, clasping the boy's hands in hers and smiling and nodding toward his mom.

"Toe guy blandgun chew fizz gloom," his grandpa said to Sam, then looked straight at Big B.

Sam nodded.

"What?" Big B asked, feeling out of the loop.

"Um, he says he wants me to show you to your room. Come on."

As they walked inside the house, the Professor suddenly yelled one coherent word: "Pirates!" But then his speech turned back into babble as he tried to talk to his daughter.

Startled, Sam and Big B looked at each other, and then Sam turned away and hurried up the porch steps. Big B moved to follow her, but his phone bleeped again.

"How could I get a text? It's turned off?" Totally confused, Big B opened the phone to reveal the same crazy image he had seen before. *Had my phone been off at the airport too?* "This thing is nuts." Big B, frustrated, gave the phone a couple of smacks against the palm of his hand as he walked up the steps. All of a sudden the screen went red, and then flickered and buzzed. The letter *F* showed up on the screen, then *I*, *N*, and *D,* and then several more letters. When the letters finished appearing in random order, they spelled the phrase *ADRIFT HE WENT.*

"What's that supposed to mean?"

"What?" asked Sam, with barely suppressed irritation.

Big B looked back at the screen, but it had gone blank. He growled in frustration and flipped his phone close.

"You're nuts, Gallo."

"Listen, if you're going to call me names, the least you could do is tell me what they mean."

Sam smirked. "*Gallo* means 'rooster.'" She put her hand over her head like a rooster's crest and wiggled her fingers. So she'd noticed his hair.

"Whatever, Grape Ape!" Big B stuck out his lip and hung his arms down in his best gorilla impersonation.

Sam rolled her eyes, turned her back on him, and walked into the house. She was waiting for Big B when he stepped inside the front door. "This is the great room. We eat over there." She pointed at a giant table on one side of the room. "The kitchen is back there." She led him out of the great room and into a long hallway. There were two doors on the left and two doors on the right. They were staggered, as if set on an invisible zigzag along the length of the passage.

"The first door on the left is your mom's room. The bathroom is here on the right and your room is the second door down on the left."

The hallway ended with a glass door that revealed a lush flower garden. The glass reflected a faint image of a second Sam and Big B approaching themselves.

"Whose room is that?" Big B asked, pointing to the last door on the right. He wondered whose room he would be sleeping across from.

"You can just forget about that room." Sam's voice sounded serious.

"Got some skeletons in the closet?" Big B teased.

Sam looked uneasy. "No. It's the Professor's study. That room is strictly off-limits, so don't even think about it!" Sam seemed to instinctively understand Big B's curious nature.

"Okay, okay. I get it."

"Well, Gallo, you're starting to smell like a rooster, thanks to that lovely hairdo, or should I say 'poo-doo'? You'd better wash up and change before dinner."

With that, Sam hurried down the hall, leaving Big B to fend for himself.

He pushed open the door to his room. It was small but pleasant, with a single bed in the corner, near a window. On the other side of the room was a dresser, a little desk with a chair, and a carved wooden lamp. Hanging from the open window was a tiny wind chime that tinkled in the breeze.

"Man, what a day!"

Once he had decided to accept Sam's unwanted advice by taking a shower and putting on clean clothes, Big B felt refreshed—but exhausted. He lay down and gently stretched out on his bed. He closed his eyes and relaxed while thinking of all that he had just experienced: A forever-long plane ride. A feisty girl with purple hair. A banana-mobile. A seagull attack. His tired body wanted him to doze off, but he could not silence his mind. His thoughts continued to race with images of the day. Eventually his mind settled for a moment on the gentle, almost hypnotizing swing of the misty Vista de los Espíritus sign.

As he was dozing off into the pleasure of an afternoon nap, a scream echoed loudly in his mind: "Pirates!"

Big B sat straight up, and the hair on the back of his neck stood on end. It was Grandpa's voice, but it was scarier than when he had heard it before, as though Grandpa were underwater, gurgling . . . drowning. Big B looked around, breathing hard.

"Grandpa?" He called out.

Nothing but silence answered back.

Chapter 4
Black gold

A loud knock startled Big B.

"Time for dinner, honey," Big B's mom called through the door.

"Coming," he shouted.

Stepping out of his room, he was enveloped by the enticing smells of dinner wafting down the hallway. His stomach rumbled.

The dining room glowed a warm orange. The long rustic table was set with fresh tropical flowers and lit by large handmade candles. A bounty of food awaited, laid out on banana leaves, wooden platters, and hollowed out pineapple halves. Big B had never smelled food quite like this or seen such exotic dishes.

"Please, sit," beckoned Rosa. Big B got the impression that Rosa smiled all the time. He liked her immediately.

Big B sat across from Sam in order to be next to his grandpa, who occupied the chair on the end. As the creator of the meal, Rosa sat at the opposite end of the table, with Armando to her left and Big B's mom to her right.

"I hope you enjoy tonight's meal," said Rosa. "*Salud!* May you glow with health!"

"Please, my friends, help yourselves!" Armando passed a platter of aromatic rice to Big B's mom.

It's a good thing I'm starving, thought Big B, his eyes wide with anticipation. Baked fish with spices and onions, slow-cooked beans, rice, fruit . . . He helped himself to a hunk of homemade bread, slathering it in fresh-churned butter and passion fruit preserves. He listened as Rosa described the salsa to his mom.

"Here on the island we call it *anuenue* salsa, which means 'rainbow, full of many colors.' Red tomatoes, yellow pineapple, orange mango, green chilies, and purple onions. Good health comes in many colors. Big B, help yourself."

Everything about dinner was amazing—until the vegetable was presented. Rosa disappeared into the kitchen for a moment and then reappeared with a tray piled high. It instantly made Big B's stomach churn: cooked green leaves.

Before he could stop himself, Big B exclaimed, "Ugh! What's that?"

"Brett! Don't be rude!"

"I'm sorry. I've just . . . um . . . never seen anything like that before."

"This is *katuk*."

"What's cat uck?"

"It's a green, leafy vegetable that grows on the island. It's incredibly nutritious." Rosa held out a scoop.

"Oh, no thanks," Big B put up a hand, "If it's green, it's not for me."

"Oh, but the katuk is fresh from Armando's hedges," pleaded Rosa. "We only serve it on special occasions."

"You better eat it, Gallo, or you'll never survive your time on the island!" Everyone except him seemed to think that was very funny. He turned red, and then made a face at her.

"Ooh, I'm scared."

"She's right, Brett—there's a reason the katuk is so popular among the locals. Legend says it makes you hearty enough to swim the oceans, strong enough to climb the mountains, and wise enough to outwit the *uhane'ino*. That means 'evil spirits,' for you newcomers," commented Professor Prune through a mouthful of dark soft leaves.

Everyone stopped and stared in shock at the Professor. A wave of relief swept the table, and Big B's mom started to say something to her dad, but his next words stopped her.

"Blark, blark," he said, looking at Big B while making a motion with his fork.

Big B had no idea if the katuk had caused the temporary clarity, but he decided to eat it just in case. "Uh, okay Grandpa." Big B took a big swallow and was pleasantly surprised by the sweetness. Plus, the katuk had a nutty flavor that was not unpleasant.

Professor Prune smiled a big green grin in response, but was quiet for the rest of the meal and didn't respond to any questions. He looked tired, as if his spirit had been drained, and he seemed lost in his own hazy world. After dinner, he muttered a few words in his slurred speech.

"Blanks door a flunderbull neal, Grossa."

"You're most welcome, Professor, I'm so glad you enjoyed it."

Professor Prune stood and wandered off toward his room.

"Off to bed, I guess." Sam's mom shrugged unhappily.

As Professor Prune turned down the hall, he began muttering to himself. As before, Big B couldn't decipher most of what his grandfather said, but he thought he heard two words clearly: "blue bones." Big B wondered what *that* was all about.

"I think I'm going to sleep early, too," said his mom. "Thank you so much for an incredible meal, Rosa. You are an amazing cook. Dad is very lucky."

"My pleasure, Angela. You sleep well. It's been a long day, I'm sure." Sam's mom turned to Sam and Big B. "How about you two helping with clean-up?"

"Sure, Mom." Sam sounded agreeable, but the sidelong glance she gave Big B told him it was grudging agreement.

Sam and Big B collected the dishes and leftovers, taking them to the kitchen. Big B found a small garbage can and began to dump scraps from the plates into it.

Sam ran over and grabbed his arm. "What are you doing!?"

"What do you mean? I'm cleaning off the plates."

"We don't throw perfectly good food away."

"Well, you aren't going to eat it off of other people's plates . . . are you?"

"Of course not. We turn it into black gold."

"What's black gold?"

"Compost. Just scrape the food into that bucket over there."

Sam packed the leftovers up and put them into the refrigerator. When everything had been put away, she grabbed the bucket of dinner scraps and a flashlight and walked toward the back door. "Come on," she called over her shoulder.

They headed downhill from the house with the round, white spot from Sam's light leading the way. The sky was full of stars, more than Big B had ever seen. Back at home the city lights and haze got in the way. The air seemed so clear on the island that Big B thought he could see for hundreds of starry miles in all directions.

They reached two rectangular structures made from black volcanic stone, each about the size of a refrigerator turned on its side. Sam handed Big B the flashlight and then lifted the wooden top of one of the boxes. Big B shone the light inside. The box was filled with pink, shiny, squirming worms and lots of leaves and grass. Sam dumped the bucket in the middle. Worms immediately began crawling all over the food, burrowing into a pile of katuk stems.

"Ee-yew! That's nasty. There must be thousands of them."

"Yeah, but without them, this world would be up to its ears in waste. That pile of food will be gone by morning."

A rumbling sound came from a pipe in the corner of the box. A little water trickled out.

"Better close it up." Sam shut the lid. "Special delivery on the way."

Big B looked clueless. "Huh?"

"Someone inside just flushed a toilet."

"No way. You mean . . ."

"Oh, yeah. It's all organic. And the more waste you put in this box, the faster they eat it."

"Now you're really grossing me out. Why don't you all do what other *civilized* people do? Ever heard of a sewage plant? Or a garbage dump."

"Sewage plants use lots and lots of energy, and they're wasteful. Energy is expensive way out here."

"Well then . . . my dad has a cabin in the mountains that uses a septic system. When you flush, it just goes into the ground, where it belongs," replied Big B, proving to Sam he knew the right answer.

"The Professor . . . your grandpa hates those. The waste is out of sight, but all the stuff in it eventually leaks out and pollutes the rivers and ocean. They call it 'nutrients.' Nutrient pollution causes bad changes in the environment. Even here on the island, it causes algae to overgrow and kill coral reefs. It happens mostly where there are lots of houses with septic tanks, and also if too much fertilizer is put on lawns or crops."

Big B heard a splash of liquid in the first box again and he winced.

"Fine, then why don't you just leave your garbage for the garbage trucks to take?"

"And what would they do with it? Dump it in a landfill somewhere, where it would sit for hundreds of years? So it could mix with poisons and leak into the soil and our water? Is that what we should do, city boy?"

"Well . . . I . . ."

Sam talked over him. "This is the natural way to get rid of our waste. When a leaf from a tree falls to the ground, or a hummingbird poops, what happens to it?"

"Well, I guess . . ."

"The insects and plants on the ground eat it up and recycle it into more life."

Sam lifted the top of the other box. The inside of this one seemed drier and smelled musty and almost sweet, like rotting leaves in the fall back home.

"This box hasn't had anything put in it for a few months, so the worms and bacteria have been breaking it down really well. Now it's super-food for plants. Next week, we'll spread it around the mango trees."

Big B heard splashing. He shined the flashlight in the direction of the sound and saw water trickling from a pipe that came out of the first box. He looked up at Sam with a raised eyebrow, as if he had found a flaw in the system, some kind of pollution that the boxes released. *Ha! It probably went into the ground.*

"And the water from these boxes goes through that pipe and is filtered through wetlands and beds of mushrooms in a greenhouse down the hill. It ends up in our ponds, clean and ready to support the fish and frogs."

Sam turned to Big B. "You city people have no idea how amazing nature is, how much it can do but how easy it is to damage. You come here with your hotels and condos and resorts and build and build . . . it makes me so *mad*."

Big B was stunned and speechless. *What is this girl's deal?* Sam turned and trotted back to the house through the dark. Big B trudged after her.

The pair continued with their kitchen chores in silence. They finished just as Sam's parents returned from locking up for the night, ready to take Sam home.

"Do you need anything before we go, Big B?" asked Rosa.

"No, I'll just watch some TV before I go to bed. By the way, where is the TV?" Big B asked looking around the great room.

"There isn't one," Sam seemed pleased to reply.

"Seriously? How can you *live* without TV?" Big B wondered aloud in horror.

"The Professor says TV is about sitting around watching other people live while your life drains out into the couch."

Big B couldn't believe this girl was his age. "It must be so boring around here, with nothing for you to do."

"Only a city boy could ever think this island is boring. It's hard to believe you are even related to the Professor. What a waste." She stopped and thought for a moment. "Not the kind even the Professor can turn into treasure." And with that she stormed out of the house.

Yeah, black gold. Real precious, thought Big B. But with nothing better to do, he turned and headed for bed.

Chapter 5
the pond monsters

Big B awoke to the cawing, croaking, and creaking music of an island morning. He had slept soundly and was ready to discover the island. But a sudden realization dampened his spirits.

The only person his age he had met so far was Sam, and she seemed to hate him. Obviously Sam would be spending a lot of time at his grandfather's house, and she might be the only non-adult around—although she sure didn't talk like one. Sam would take some figuring out.

He jumped out of bed and threw on some shorts, a Bent Lizard T-shirt, and his wrestling shoes. He grabbed his phone—it was evidently worthless here, but he felt naked without it. And just in case it did start to work, he didn't want to miss a call from his dad or a message from Jack.

Rosa was in the kitchen cleaning vegetables. "Good morning, Big B."

"Hi."

"Are you hungry?"

"Yeah, always."

"Well, there's fruit salad in the refrigerator and eggs, fresh from our chickens, on the stove."

"Great, thanks." Big B fixed himself a plate of food and sat at the kitchen table. Without looking at Rosa, he asked, "Where's Sam? Did she go to school?"

"No. School on the island ended last week. It's officially summer now. Sam's helping her dad with some plants in the front yard. She inherited her father's love of all things green. I think that's why she's so devoted to your grandfather. He does so much to protect the island."

"What do you mean?"

"His inventions help protect the environment here and he has fought developers whose plans threatened some of the most fragile parts of the island, like the coral reefs and the rain forests."

Big B wondered how his grandfather would be able to keep up his work if he could barely talk. He took a last bite of egg, thanked Rosa, and went outside to find Sam.

Armando and Sam were standing over a hole in the yard.

"Good morning, Big B. Sam and I were just discussing your predicament," said Armando.

"My what?"

"Your problem."

"What problem?"

"Well, the island is a bit different from Chicago. You might need some help discovering all of the fun things there are to do here."

It was obvious to Big B that Sam was making a point not to look at him.

"Sam, why don't you give Big B a tour? You can learn a lot from this *chica*, Mr. B. No one knows the secrets of this place better than Sam."

"Umm . . . that would be great."

"Yeah, I could do that," said Sam nonchalantly.

"I should tell my mom where I'm going."

"She's in the backyard with the Professor. I'll let her know." Armando waved them off with a grin.

"Come on then," said Sam.

Big B felt a little apprehensive—a feeling he wasn't used to—and he looked at Sam with uncertainty.

"Come on, don't be a *pollo*. The island won't eat you," Sam snapped.

"Po-yo?"

"Chicken."

"It's not the island I'm afraid of." Big B looked at her warily.

Sam laughed and took off, disappearing into a dense growth of trees.

Man, she's fast, Big B thought as he charged after her. He tightened his grip on his cell phone as he entered the trees, dodging from left to right, just like in football practice, but now avoiding branches and bushes, not other players. He could hear her laughing just ahead of him, but he couldn't yet see her. He was one of the fastest guys on the football team, but he couldn't catch this girl.

"Over here, Pollo!"

"I'll show her chicken," Big B muttered, gritting his teeth and digging hard into the soft earth with his feet. His wrestling shoes connected his feet to the ground, letting him grip every stone and root. He saw an opening ahead where Sam must have darted out of the trees. He blocked the branches with his arms as he broke out of the foliage and into the light.

Suddenly, the ground beneath him disappeared but his feet kept running through the wide-open air. In the corner of his eye, he saw Sam giggling in the distance as he flew forward, his hair rippling with the speed. When he looked down again, he saw a flat shiny surface waiting below him. In a fraction of a second, he reacted and tossed his phone back behind him like a perfect pitch in football, just before his body crashed into . . . water. Very cold water.

Desperately, he thrust his legs down, pushed against a mucky but solid bottom, and rocketed to the surface. The air hit his lungs and he coughed, spitting out water. He was breathing rapidly, his heart in his throat.

Sam was kneeling at the pond's edge, laughing at him. With his red hair matted down over his face, he looked pitiful and knew it. She yelled at him, "Pollo! Looks like you put out your own fire!"

Big B flipped his matted hair back into its crest. "Man, why did you do that? These are my favorite shoes! And where's my phone?" He spoke in near panic.

"Oh, your precious phone." She spotted it lying a few feet away and called to him, "It's safe, Pollo."

"Good," he called back, still treading water. But then he started to slap and thrash. "Hey, stop! Ouch! Something's biting me!"

"Those are fish, silly. They must be hungry," Sam offered calmly. She noted that Big B looked gratifyingly fearful.

"Relax, they're strictly vegetarian," she said, adding smugly, "Too bad! But see here."

Sam shook one of the trees, making seedpods fall into the pond. The fish came to the surface to gobble them up.

Curious, Big B took a deep breath and sank beneath the water to get a good look at the pond monsters. It was surprisingly quiet, especially after his serious plunge. He slowly opened his eyes. In the dark, murky water, he saw the fish turn to look back at him, the strange-looking red-headed seed pod.

He wasn't really comfortable in the water, but only he knew that. Water always seemed so mysterious. There was so much beneath the surface that you couldn't see, and what you could see was strange, almost alien, like outer space. But now, with all the eyes looking at him, he almost forgot that he was underwater.

Just as he was beginning to enjoy the soothing calm of this different world, he felt his skull pendant being pulled gently away from him. He looked down as it extended away from his body, expecting to see a fish nibbling on the leather string . . . but there was nothing there. The eyes of the skull seemed to glow. Confused, he felt his heart beat faster. He reached out for the pendant, but something blocked his hand. He froze and suddenly what felt like a hand grabbed his own hand and squeezed it tightly. The sensation lasted only a second or two, until fear shot Big B to the surface. He gasped for air as he scrambled out of the water and onto the bank, where Sam sat waiting.

"What's wrong, afraid of the fish?"

Big B tucked the pendant under his shirt. "No. No I just . . . I just swallowed some water."

In the bright sunlight, he wasn't sure what he had seen or felt. *It couldn't have been a hand. It was just some underwater plant that I got caught in.* He didn't really believe that, but what he had felt didn't make sense.

"As I was trying to explain, the trees feed the fish and the fish feed us," Sam chattered, interrupting Big B's confused thoughts. "And once in a while we scoop the mud from the bottom and flush it down those canals over there into the garden down below. It's a bit stinky, but it makes my tomatoes grow huge . . . and fast. Pretty cool, huh?"

"What? Well, I don't know. I guess it's . . ."

Sam kept talking over the questions racing through his head. "The Professor designed the whole place as an ecosystem. It's all interconnected. Come on, you can see more up here." She took off running again.

Big B cast one last glance at the dark surface of the water before chasing after Sam.

Chapter 6
The Vista

Big B followed Sam as she ran off along the edge of the pond and up a hill behind it, following the waterfall. She bounced across rocks, hopped over little streams, and dodged between bushes and trees and grasses of every size, shape, and color. He pushed away his fear with logic, just as he did on the field when he was facing down some huge linebacker. What happened in the pond was perfectly reasonable. Of course, it was a fish. It was probably attracted to the shiny silver necklace. *Dude, sometimes you are crazy,* he told himself, wondering if it ran in his family.

He saw Sam scrambling nimbly over a big black lava outcropping and park herself on a point of rock overlooking the valley and the harbor beyond. Her agility was impressive. He climbed up and dropped next to her. Spray from the waterfall that cascaded alongside blew lightly across them. He noticed that she wasn't breathing hard at all, even after what he thought was a serious run and climb.

"Welcome to The Vista. It gives the farm its name."

"Let's go higher. I want to see where all this water comes from," Big B said, trying to prove he wasn't tired.

"Oh, it comes from way up in the volcano forest, in the clouds; that's why the water's cold. It's incredible up there, but what I think is just as amazing is where it goes. Down there. See."

Big B looked out across the valley below them. He could see the ocean far off on the horizon. Scattered across the valley floor were fields of crops, ponds, canals, windmills, and buildings, all surrounded by thick green forests.

A tiny metallic-blue body buzzed around them, sparkling like fireworks on the Fourth of July. It bobbed in and out of the flowers that thrived near the waterfall. It hovered right in front of Big B as if he were a gigantic red flower, and then darted off through the mist.

"Red-headed hummingbird," Sam said, in case he didn't know. *Purple-headed troublemaker*, thought Big B. But the vista from The Vista took his breath away.

"Wow. It's so . . . so . . ." Big B struggled to find words to describe the view.

"It's *palekaiko*."

"Right. Pal-eh-kay-ko."

"Paradise." Sam wanted to be sure Big B understood what he was looking at, besides how lovely it was. "It's all about the water. The Professor calls it a water web and my dad calls it the lifeblood of the farm, but it's just a gift. From nature, from the forest up there. See the canals running through the orchards? Those fluffy green trees are banana trees. Then the water runs to the algae ponds. And some goes to the digester."

Big B wondered why algae were such a big deal on this farm.

"You can feed algae to fish, you can fertilize the gardens with it, and if you have any left you can run a truck with it!"

"So your dad was being serious when he said the Cruiser could run on algae?"

"You got here from the airport on bananas, Pollo. We turn bananas into ethanol in that long, low building over there. And, we can turn algae into ethanol, too. Ethanol is a liquid and goes right into the fuel tank on the Cruiser. Anyway, then the water from the algae ponds goes to the fish ponds. You already know about fish ponds, right?" She glanced slyly at his still-dripping clothes.

Changing the subject, Big B asked, "What's the digester?"

"It's those domes over there," Sam explained. "We can also turn algae and other plants into biogas. Biogas really is a gas, not a liquid like the ethanol. We mix up all kinds of plant parts, and . . . um . . . poop from the animals."

"Ee-yew. That's gross."

"It's just manure. Haven't you ever been on a farm before?"

Big B shrugged his shoulders.

"Trust me. It's no big deal. Bacteria in the digester turns it into a gas that can be burned. Biogas. The gas is used to run the stove, fruit driers, and even the Professor's Bunsen burners in his lab. He calls it the *real* natural gas."

"Like burning farts," joked Big B.

Sam rolled her eyes. "Nothing here is wasted." The Professor . . . your grandpa . . . modeled it all after the way nature does things. He says nature is the real genius if we can just watch, listen, and learn."

"Can he fix my cell phone reception? I barely got one bar the whole drive out here. If you put a cell tower up here, you could get great reception in the whole valley. Speaking of which . . ."

Big B held out an open hand.

Sam rolled her eyes again and dug in her pocket for his phone.

"This thing beeps too much." As if to confirm what Sam had said, the phone beeped again. At the same moment Sam's amulet flashed red. They exchanged glances.

"Maybe this time it's a real message," said Big B, as he flipped the phone open. "Ahh. No bars up here either. But how come I keep getting this crazy picture? It's just jumbled, warped words, symbols, and smudgy colors. How am I supposed to stay in touch with the world with my phone all screwed up?"

"Look around you, Gallo. You are in touch with the world." Sam spread her arms out wide.

"Yeah, whatever. And quit calling me Gallo."

"Do you really think I'm going to call you 'Big B'?"

"That's what my friends call me."

"Why?"

"Just because."

"Well, if you don't tell me, I'm going to keep calling you Gallo." Sam sat down on the edge of the overlook, legs crossed.

Big B heaved a frustrated sigh. They stared silently at the view until Big B couldn't stand it. "Fine. My real name is Brett, but my friends started calling me 'The Big B' about a year ago and it just stuck."

"But why?" Sam looked at him.

"I thought it was because I am bigger than they are, but that's not what they meant." He kicked a rock off the cliff. "It's because I usually bomb. To them, B stands for *bomb*."

"What?"

"You know. When I try new things, like a new trick on my board, I usually wipe out or mess things up. Last week in Mr. Gruber's science lab, they had to clear out the whole room because my experiment caused such a mess—and a really bad smell. I'm usually pretty good at science, and math too. I don't know what happened. Mr. Gruber gave me a D for not following directions. My best friend, Jack, laughed his butt off. He called me 'The Stink Bomb.'"

Big B felt a little embarrassed revealing all this, but for once, Sam didn't tease him. To break the silence, he asked, "So why do they call you Sam?"

"Actually my real name is Sarita Araceli Morales Flores, but my friends just call me Sam for short."

"Sam's a cool name for a girl," he said.

Sam didn't say anything. Big B could tell the subject was closed. She closed her eyes and breathed in deep and slow, as though he weren't even there.

Big B thought maybe he'd said something wrong.

"The Vista is my meditation place."

"Meditation?"

"I just go inside myself and be quiet. It's what I do when I need a break from squawking chickens," Sam said, turning toward him.

"Ha!" Big B said defensively. "I've barely gotten a word in edgewise with you yammering all morning!"

"Oh, please." She crossed her arms and looked out to the horizon. "The Vista is my favorite spot. There is just no better place to just sit quietly and think."

"About what?"

"Things that are going on. People I know. Stuff that makes me happy. And stuff I don't tell anybody about."

"Yeah, like what?"

"Big B. Really. Don't you listen at all? You should give it a try. But we're here, so go on, close your eyes. Bring your hands together at your heart and breathe in very very deeply."

Big B breathed an unhappy sigh. He realized that there was no arguing with Sam. He took a more relaxed, serious breath, and then closed his eyes. After a minute of silence, when he couldn't resist opening one eye a little to peek at Sam, something caught his peripheral vision.

Big B looked out at the horizon. He thought he saw a sailboat gliding across the slice of ocean that the mouth of the valley revealed. He opened both eyes and squinted to see it more clearly. It was kind of hard to see at that distance. Plus a fog had rolled in over the ocean and breaking waves kicked up a misty haze.

It was a sailboat, but not like the bright white boat he had seen from the plane. This one was dark, with three masts and dirty-grey, tattered sails. But it was hard to tell through the shroud of murky fog. He squinted harder and saw a flag flying at the top of the biggest mast. Is that what he thought it was? No, it couldn't be. It looked like a pirate flag, black with maybe a white skull and crossbones.

"Hey! Look." He nudged Sam.

"Stop it." She pushed him back, hard.

Big B fell to the side, knocking a pebble over the ledge. He watched with wide eyes as the pebble fell a long, long way down.

"Hey! Not cool!"

"Oops. I didn't mean to freak you out."

"You didn't."

"Seriously. I apologize. Meditation is supposed to improve the way you behave. What was it you wanted to show me?"

He looked back out at the ocean. The ship was gone.

Chapter 7
the Stone of Souls

I t was nothing. Just a . . . boat. It must have sailed behind those rocks."

Sam gave him an odd look, then stood up.

Big B stood up taller. He kicked another rock off the cliff and watched it plunk into a clear pool far below them. "Hey, I'm hungry."

"I guess we'd better head home for lunch. Follow me and I'll get you a little snack along the way," Sam said, leading the way down from the ledge.

"You got a candy bar or something?"

"No, something much better, I promise," Sam answered cheerfully.

She swiftly led him back down through the wooded path. Big B and his grumbling stomach followed close behind, his shorts, still wet, sticking to his legs. He paused at the fish pond, considering the dark glassy surface. *It was just weeds.*

About halfway back to the house, Sam made a quick right turn up a slope onto a dry, sandy outcrop full of cactuses and surrounded by tall, thin palm trees. By the time he had climbed the slope, she had already scrambled high up into the canopy of one of the trees.

Suddenly something small and hard bounced off Big B's head. *Ping!*

"Ow! Hey, quit it, you psycho spider monkey!"

"Catch, Gallo! Here chick, chick, chicken. Come eat your snack!"

Ping! Ping! Ping! Three more flying objects rained down on Big B's head.

"Hey! What are you throwing at me! Monkey poo?" He rubbed his head and picked up the small brown objects. "Nasty! It *is* monkey poo, all brown and wrinkly. Gross!"

"They're dates, silly. Try one!" encouraged Sam as she shimmied down the tall trunk.

He frowned at the fruit. Sam snatched one out of his hand and took a bite. "I'll take the rest of those if you're too afraid." Big B smiled rebelliously and popped the whole fruit into his mouth, filling it with sugary sweetness.

"Wow, these are really good!" He spat out the pit and then popped two more into his mouth, savoring the rich flavor.

"Yep, nature's candy," said Sam as she ate another. "A lot better for you than most of the garbage you can buy at the store."

As Big B chewed, he absentmindedly pulled the pendant out from under his shirt and rolled it around in his fingers.

"Wh-where did you get that?" Sam shuddered as she spoke.

"This?" Big B held up the cylinder between his thumb and finger. "My grandpa. I got it just before we left to come here. Cool, huh?"

Sam didn't respond. The stone in her amulet began pulsing red, reminding Big B of a heartbeat. He was mesmerized by the color. His phone beeped but he ignored it.

"What about *your* necklace? Where'd you get it?"

"It's not a necklace, it's an amulet—and it has special powers."

Big B tried his best not to laugh.

"No, seriously. It's called the Stone of Souls and it's a family heirloom."

"The Stone of Souls? What's that supposed to mean?"

"Do you really want to hear the story?"

"Yeah. Tell me."

"Okay, then." Sam took a deep breath. "My ancestors go back four hundred years on this island, beginning with a woman named Isabella who was shipwrecked. Some Nui Islander fishermen found her floating on a plank. I call her my grandmother, *mi abuela*, but of course she's that a gazillion times over."

"How do you know that?" Big B asked, skeptically. "That was a long time ago."

"The people on this island know history that goes a lot farther back than that," Sam replied. "Anyway, she was Peruvian, and was a captive on a Spanish ship, and other Spanish merchant ships besides the one she was on came and went a lot back then, so that's why we speak Spanish." She looked at him for signs of comprehension.

"But what does that have to do with the charm, the amulet?"

Patiently, Sam continued. "Okay, when you've been floating around on a plank for a few days in the open water, you are not in good shape, right? So the fishermen took her to the village *kahuna*, the healer, to make her well again. She learned a lot about healing from the kahuna, besides what she already knew from growing up in Peru."

"And . . . ?" Big B hated long stories.

"And later on, when foreign ships started bringing strange diseases to the island, mi abuela knew how to help the sick people. She defended them from the illnesses that came with the *haole*."

"The what?"

"Haole, foreigners. People like you—and me, as far as that goes. So anyway the villagers were so grateful to her that they gave her, ta-da!" and Sam swung the jewel happily before his eyes. "The Stone of Souls! It has been worn by one kahuna after another for centuries. Kahunas are always women," she added, somewhat smugly.

"Does that make you a kahuna?" Big B had to ask.

"Maybe. Maybe someday." Sam was suddenly serious. "So listen up. I think you should know why the Stone of Souls is so powerful. The island people say it comes from Magma herself, the all-powerful Earth Mother. The story says she gave it to her daughters, the island's three volcanoes. First to her eldest, Ho'okano, the tallest and most proud. Then to the middle, Na'au, filled with fiery passions. And finally, to the smallest and youngest of the sisters, Makemake, keeper of dreams and wishes. It was at the foot of this volcano, deposited by a flowing stream of lava, where the Stone of Souls was first discovered. The stone has been handed down from mother to daughter for many, many years. Eventually, it came to my great-great-many-greats grandmother and now, fifteen generations later, it is mine to care for." Sam smiled with pride. The amulet glowed red under her smile.

Big B laughed. "Are you serious? That's like a total chick fest! Cool story, though, for a fancy mood ring." His phone beeped as if to accentuate his amusement. "Did you know that it probably works because of your body heat?"

Sam's smile disappeared. "I knew you wouldn't believe me!" She spat a date pit at Big B and it bounced off his ear. Before he could open his mouth to yell, she disappeared through the ferns like a startled deer.

Here we go again, he thought, sprinting back down the path after her. Suddenly, his phone beeped again and then emitted a series of strange tones, which made Big B stop. He pulled the phone from his pocket and flipped it open. Instead of the crazy warped image, he got the same strange letter-by-letter text as yesterday, when he arrived at the house. First an *F*, then *I*, *N*, *D*, *T*, followed by several more letters. The letters abruptly scrambled their order, again spelling the words *ADRIFT HE WENT.*

Chapter 8
the Captain's Log

"Scram scobble krill." Grandpa sang out as Sam and Big B raced toward the house. At the last second Big B caught up to Sam, and they leaped onto the porch at the same time. Big B collapsed onto a bamboo bench, breathing hard. He looked at Sam for an interpretation of his grandfather's words, but Sam only shrugged her shoulders.

Professor Prune said nothing more to them and just walked around the corner of the house and out of sight. "Poor Grandpa," Big B said, sadly.

"He'll be okay," Sam reassured him, but she didn't look convinced. "Come on, let's get something to drink."

Inside the house it was cool, comfortable, and a bit breezy.

"It's a lot cooler in here than outside. How come I don't hear the air conditioner?" Big B looked around for vents, but didn't see any.

"There isn't one," said Rosa, coming in from the kitchen. "The Professor designed the house so that it would be cooled naturally. The breezes from the ocean are funneled toward the house by the trees out front. The air comes through all of the windows on that side of the house, passes by the water wall over there, and blows out the windows over there." Rosa made an arc with her hand as she spoke and went back to her chores.

Big B had seen the stone wall with water running over it the night before, but he had thought it was just there for decoration.

"That water comes from an underground spring, so it's very cold. It cools the air around it. And those holes in the ceiling are like chimneys that let heat escape out the top of the house."

"I can't believe he created all this stuff. He can barely talk."

"He hasn't always been like that, you know," Sam said. "It just started a few weeks ago."

"What happened?" asked Big B.

"We don't know. He just stumbled into the house late one night. He was all scraped up and wet from the rain, and he was talking nonsense. We took him to the hospital and they thought he had had a stroke, but they couldn't find anything wrong with him. After a day or so, they let us take him home."

"He's lucky you guys were here," said Big B, suddenly appreciating how important Sam's family was to his grandfather.

"Yeah, I guess..."

Big B thought that Sam wanted to say something more, but she seemed more interested in what was going on in the kitchen. Rosa was preparing lunch. That interested Big B, too.

"Hey, Mom, you need any help?"

"No, thanks, sweetie. Lunch is about ready. But you guys look thirsty. Here." She poured them each a glass of a light yellow liquid from a pitcher. "Have some water."

"Yum," said Big B, licking it off his lips. "Is this some kind of special Nui Island water?" He drained his glass then tried to shake one more drop out of the upturned glass.

"Ice cold water with a splash of fresh-squeezed pineapple and lemon juice … and a green tea extract that your grandpa makes." Rosa refilled his glass. "Sit down. I made you two some fish tacos with anuenue salsa."

"That looks awesome!" said Big B, attacking the plate of food Rosa had placed on the table in front of him. "Do you have more dates? We just had some, right off the tree."

"Well, in that case, you better munch on these, too." Sam's mom threw them two large carrots from a bowl on the counter.

"Carrots?"

"Nature's toothbrush," Sam said, rolling her eyes. "Thanks, Mom," she said sarcastically.

"Dates are delicious, but sweet and sticky. You two munch on those carrots to save those smiles!" Rosa said, flashing her extra-white, beautiful teeth.

"So, what's for dinner tonight?" Big B managed to ask while stuffing almost an entire fish taco in his mouth.

Rosa answered from the kitchen, "Pollo!"

Sam burst into laughter and pointed gleefully at Big B, as bits of rainbow salsa sprayed out of her mouth and into the air. Big B couldn't help laughing too. Once they had cleared their plates from their messy lunch, Sam grabbed Big B by the wrist and pulled him to the door. "Come on, Gallo, let's go see what my dad is doing."

They found Armando harvesting vegetables in a garden not far from the house. They spent the rest of the afternoon digging and pulling up dead plants and then planting new ones. As they worked, Armando explained how he had helped the Professor create the gardens, the composting system, and the water treatment system. He described the connection he felt to the land, the magic it held for him.

Big B couldn't believe how much fun he was having working in a garden. When it was finally time for dinner, he was ravenous.

As promised, they had delicious chicken for dinner. Big B filled his plate twice, and he even asked for katuk, which made everybody laugh. He and Sam helped clean up again, and suddenly the day was over. Sam left with her parents, and Big B headed for bed.

Exhausted, he fell back onto his pillow, but instead of a soft landing, his head thumped something hard. "Ow!"

He sat up and squeezed the pillow. It was soft and downy, not hard at all. Big B rubbed the back of his head, puzzled. He turned the pillow over to fluff it, but, in midflip, he saw what he'd knocked his head on.

Underneath his pillow lay an old, tattered, leather-bound book. It smelled like dust, mold, and seawater. He read the words on the cover, whispering them out loud: "Captain's Log . . . *The Bloodlust.*" Embossed into the leather was the Jolly Roger, a menacing skull and crossbones.

"Pirates," he whispered. The mysteries it had to contain—to say nothing of the mystery of how it got under his pillow—shut out every other thought. For a minute or two he just sat on the edge of his bed with the old book on his lap, savoring the prospect of learning what it could teach him.

A light rain started to fall outside. He could smell it in the air and hear the light pitter-patter of soft rain blowing in the wind. The wind chime tinkled a suddenly haunting sound that made him feel uneasy. A misty spray blew through the window, sprinkling him with coolness. A shiver ran down his spine.

He picked up the ship's log and flipped through the yellow, brittle pages. On the first page was a sketch of a boat. It looked like the one he had seen that morning out on the ocean. He turned the page and discovered a note written in spidery black ink:

> HE WHO DOES ATTAIN THIS TEXT, STRAIGHT AWAY CEDE TO ME, OR ACCOST THE KISS OF MY CUTLASS.
>
> SIR WILLIAM SNEATH
> CAPTAIN, THE BLOODLUST

Big B's heart beat faster. The tiny droplets of water from the misty rain that were drifting in through the open window collected on his furrowed forehead. They merged together into one large drop, which slid down the length of his nose and fell with a plop onto the yellowed page of Captain Sneath's ship's log. It landed directly on the *Sn* in *Sneath*. Big B tried to rub off the water, but smeared the letters. He rubbed it some more with his shirt.

"Oh, no."

He tried to dry it by blowing on it, but it was already ruined. Big B examined the damage and froze. The two letters that he smudged were transformed into a warped circle, forming a distorted letter *D*. The passage was now signed, *Sir William Death*.

Big B quickly closed the book and put it on the small table by his bed. He got under the covers and reached over to turn off the light, but could not stop staring at the book. He felt as though the skull and crossbones were looking back at him. Remembering his suitcase parked in the corner, Big B grabbed the pirate's journal, hopped out of bed, unzipped the suitcase, put the pirate's journal inside, and jumped back into bed. Feeling a little better, he turned out the light and lay there, slowly drifting off to sleep. But his sleep wasn't restful—images of ships, skulls, and glowing stones filled his dreams.

Chapter 9
the Legend of Ratbeard

In the morning, Big B found Sam in the kitchen eating breakfast. "So what are we going to do today?" he asked, as he spread jam around on a piece of bread.

"I don't know. How about going down to the beach?"

"Yeah, that sounds awesome."

"We can swim and check out the sailboats. Have you ever surfed?"

"Uh . . . no." Big B was distracted by the mention of boats. He started thinking about the strange book he had found under his pillow.

As soon as Rosa left the kitchen to empty the scrap bucket into the compost boxes, Big B leaned toward Sam. "Hey, can I ask you something?"

"I don't know, can you?" mocked Sam.

"No, really, come on. This is serious."

"Okay. Yeah, what is it?"

"Well . . . I found this weird book in my room last night."

"Good, you found it."

"You know about it?"

"Yeah, I left it there."

"You did? When?"

"Before dinner. When I saw your skull pendant yesterday, I figured you'd better know who it came from and what it might mean."

"This?" Big B held out the shiny cylinder.

"Yeah. I think the book's connected to what's happened to the Professor."

"What do you mean? Isn't he just sick?"

"No, I don't think so. I think it's something much worse."

"Really, what? Tell me what's going on."

Sam hesitated and looked out the window at her mom walking back toward the house. She started to speak, then stopped and looked at him doubtfully.

"Come on, tell me."

"All right." Sam lowered her voice to a whisper. "I think the Bone Pirates have captured your grandpa's spirit."

"The *what* pirates?"

"Shhhhh! Be quiet," Sam whispered.

"*Who's* cursed him?"

She glanced out the window again. "I'll explain outside."

Sam led him out onto a porch, across the yard, and into the trees. They walked up the hill to a rocky outcropping where a miniature waterfall splashed into a little pool. The tall plants growing around the waterfall hid them from the sun. Sam sat down cross-legged next to the pool on a patch of moss, and Big B sat facing her.

"So?" Big B looked at her impatiently, eyebrows raised.

Sam took a deep breath. "Promise to believe me this time?"

"Come on, tell me!"

Sam relented and began telling a story she obviously knew well. "Okay, so . . . long ago pirates sailed the seas around Nui Island. They roamed the Pacific attacking ships that sailed the trade route between Mexico and the Orient, loaded down with treasures. One of the worst pirates was Captain William Sneath."

"That's the guy's name in the book!"

"You know about Queen Elizabeth, don't you? The first one?"

"Sure. Red hair. Big dresses."

"Right. End of sixteenth century, start of the seventeenth. Well, she hired pirates! They called them privateers, but basically they were just bandits on the water. Privateers like Sir Francis Drake did their pirating for the Queen."

Big B was getting impatient. "What does that have to do with Sneath?"

"I'm getting to that. Okay, the legend has it that Sneath sailed with Drake as his cryptographer. He wrote the codes. But he wanted his own ship to command. And wanted to be like Drake—so much so that he tried to grow a beard like Drake's. Sneath wasn't a good beard-grower and it came in all scraggly and sparse, like rat whiskers. Drake ridiculed Sneath about his beard in front of the crew, calling him 'Ratbeard.'"

"Oh, I get it. That explains one thing, at least."

"Well! Sneath was not a guy who handled humiliation very well, so he jumped ship and vowed vengeance and got his own ship. It was black, made from the hardest wood in the world, from the Philippines. Iron-wood. Cannonballs just bounced off it."

"How did he do that?"

Sam gave him an exasperated look. "How should I know? It's a legend. It happened four hundred years ago. But we know he was very bad, and he was here on Nui Island. The local people pass stories like that from generation to generation. Everybody knows about his black ship, the *Bloodlust*. Sneath did terrible things, like holding its screaming captain by his beard, only to cut off the envied hair with one swipe of his cutlass, dropping the captain into the murderous ocean below. He eventually became the most feared pirate of the Pacific, acquiring vast amounts of wealth."

"So what does this story have to do with Grandpa?" Big B was clueless.

"Get this. The legend says that Ratbeard and his crew buried their treasures right here on Nui Island."

"No way!" Big B exclaimed, now hanging onto Sam's every word.

"Way." Sam took a breath then continued. "After raiding the trade ships for several months, Ratbeard returned to Nui to hide his newly acquired plunder. However, as luck would have it, after drifting windless for weeks and weeks on the open ocean with the men even starving, a huge hurricane set in and wrecked the *Bloodlust* on a reef right off the island. The pirates managed to swim to shore, but they eventually died, presumably from scurvy."

"What's scurvy?"

"Sailors used to get it when they were at sea too long without any vitamin C from fruits and vegetables. Ratbeard's crew was very sick, their wounds wouldn't heal, their teeth fell out . . ."

"So they all died?"

"Every one, including Sneath. He never got off the island. Seeing that his own end was near, he devised a plan using the bones of his crew to protect his treasure. Nobody knows what island magic he used, but the legend says he cursed their bones so that if someone happened to disturb them, the pirates would awaken, hungry for life, and begin to prey upon the souls of the living.

Big B shivered. "Wow."

"The legend says that if they gain enough life energy, they will raise their ship from the depths of the ocean, reclaim their treasure, and terrorize the seas once again." Sam's voice sunk into a quiet whisper for emphasis. "The locals call them the Bone Pirates."

"Wait. Is that what you think happened to Grandpa? You think he disturbed the pirate's bones and got the curse?"

"Exactly."

"Sam. It's just a story. A good one maybe, but definitely just a story." Big B laughed, feeling himself relax.

"It isn't *just* a story! And the ship's log, Ratbeard's journal, confirms it."

Big B stopped laughing, remembering the name, Sir William Death.

"The Professor discovered the *Bloodlust*'s log about a month ago, while excavating some island pottery in a cave near Ma'ema'e Reef. He got really excited. He had found Ratbeard's encrypted clues to the treasures. He couldn't stop talking about the legend—at least to me. He gave it to me to read. He really needs our help, Pollo."

Big B could only blink and nod. This was getting serious.

"He pointed out Ratbeard's last entry, the challenge: Anybody intelligent enough to decode his clever encryption would earn the right to his treasures and to the secrets of his magic. Your grandfather became totally obsessed by the Ratbeard legend."

"Why?"

"He can't stand not knowing the truth about things in the past especially if it can help us solve the problems of our future. He loves this island and will do whatever it takes to protect it."

"Even lose his mind to a bunch of dead pirates?"

"Even that—but that's why we need to solve Ratbeard's codes somehow so we can break the curse, stop the pirates, and . . ."

"And find the treasure." Big B grinned as he completed Sam's sentence. He didn't know if what Sam said was true—the whole thing sounded a little crazy—but he had experienced some weird stuff since he arrived on the island. He turned to look into the little pool, straining to see the bottom. The water, shaded by the trees, was dark, and he couldn't see past his own reflection in the surface. A red leaf floated through the air and landed on the water, covering his chin in the reflection. It looked like a flaming-red goatee.

The surface of the water stirred and rippled around the leaf, making the reflection of his face shift and dance. It reminded him of what it looked like when heat waves rose off a hot black road, a mirage. It made him look kind of wrinkly and much older. As the reflection wavered, the corners of the mouth began to creep up, the grin exposing dark teeth. Big B leaped up and away from the water as fear electrified his body.

It wasn't his face in the reflection. He hadn't smiled at all.

Chapter 10
ΠΛLU

What's wrong?" asked Sam, her face revealing her surprise.
Big B quickly changed his expression. "Uh . . . nothing. I
think . . . I think a bug bit me."

"Okay. So what do you think?"

"About what?"

"About the legend!"

"It sounds cool. We should definitely try to find the treasure."

"Weren't you listening? If we disturb the bones, we could have our
souls stolen! That's probably what happened to your grandpa."

"Well then, what should we do, Einstein?"

"I don't know. Maybe finding the bones is the only way to help the
Professor. I think we need to know more about what the Professor

found. We need to get into his study and look for any clues that might help us figure out how to find the bones and break the curse."

"Okay, when?"

"Tonight, after dinner."

"Fine. Can we get out of here?"

"Yeah, okay." Sam gave him a questioning look, but he just turned and ran through the trees and down the hill.

When they got back to the house, they packed some food for lunch, changed into their swimsuits, and left for the beach. Outside in the warm sun, Sam broke into a jog, following the path through the garden. They trotted downhill along the tree-shaded path. The plants growing around them changed as the ground beneath them turned sandier. Big B could hear the surf roaring ahead. The air had changed from thick and humid to light, fresh, and cool.

Big B followed Sam out of the trees and onto the beach. The bright white sand backed by the electric blue of the ocean was mesmerizing. He paused just long enough to remove his shoes and then walked past Sam onto what felt like powdered sugar. He was drawn to the water— all that blue. He felt small—very small—confronted by the endless sea. He walked to the edge of the water and stopped, silent and still.

"Welcome to Palekaiko Cove." Sam smiled as she stepped up next to him. "It's the most beautiful beach on the island. The water is really clear and clean here, thanks to the farm above. The wastewater web that the Professor and my dad created in the valley protects the cove."

Big B didn't hear a word, his attention drawn completely to the ocean ahead.

Sam poked him. "Come on, Gallo, I'm starving!"

She trotted back up the beach, pulled a woven grass mat from her backpack, and spread their lunch on it: macadamia nut muffins, hard-boiled eggs, and a glass bottle of green liquid.

Big B sat in the sand next to her. "Remember what I said about green food?"

"And didn't you enjoy it?" Sam poured him a glass. "This is even better."

Big B hesitantly took a sip of the green sludge. He was surprised.

"Hmm. This is good."

"Yeah, it's a banana, mango, and pineapple smoothie"

"Then why is it green like moldy soup?"

"I put some spirulina in it."

"Spiru-what?"

"Spear-u-lee-na. It's algae."

"Ee-yew. Like in the fish pond? That's nasty."

"Whatever. The Professor says that NASA is going to grow spirulina during long space missions to provide food for the astronauts."

"Really?" Big B looked closer at his cup.

"Yep. It's loaded with vitamins, minerals, and protein. They call it a superfood. You'd better drink it all. You're going to need the extra protein."

"Why?" asked Big B before he took a big gulp of smoothie.

"To keep away the sugar sharks!" Sam replied, widening her eyes.

"What, another nutrition lesson? Okay, Professor Purple, lay it on me."

"No, really. There are sharks out there that can smell the sugar in your blood stream." Sam looked very concerned, and Big B started to believe her.

"Serious?" He considered Jack's drawing, now fading on his arm.

"No, not really," laughed Sam. "I'm just kidding. But if you don't get enough protein, you can really bonk out there. And you don't want to lose all your energy when you're looking up at the face of a fifteen-footer."

"A fifteen-foot shark?" Big B scanned the water for fins, but all he could see was an orange-haired surfer riding a wave.

"No, Pollo, a wave. You've got to respect the wave. If you don't respect it, it can pack more power than a hungry shark."

Big B looked out at the ocean. The white, breaking edge of the waves moved as if alive, from left to right, sliding closer to shore. A wave rose and arched up into an aquamarine curl. It looked so magnificent, so compelling, and inviting. He was torn. He had an urge to charge out there, into the sparkling waves, but his fear held him back. Just in front of the breaking edge, the wave curled over into a perfect tube. Big B was amazed by its symmetry, the perfect geometry. It advanced, charging ahead to meet the sea floor rising from below, churning and tumbling. Eventually, it relaxed and settled into a frothing brew that washed up onto the sand. *SShhhhhh!*

Big B studied the surfer while he munched on a muffin.

"Who's he?" he asked Sam, pointing toward the water.

"Oh, that's Nalu," Sam said. "He shreds! He and I learned to surf together. This cove is one of his favorite spots when the waves are *nunui*—'awesome.' He surfs all around this island."

Big B remembered seeing an orange-haired surfer from the plane. *So that was Nalu,* he thought.

"Cool, I'd like to meet him!"

"Well, here he comes."

The darkly tanned surfer was paddling in through the white froth. He emerged from the surf, carrying his orange board and dripping with salt water. He revealed a bright white gleam of teeth when he recognized Sam.

"*Aloha E ke kaikamahine poni!*" he yelled over the crash of the waves.

"What does that mean?" asked Big B.

"'What's up, Purple Girl?'" Sam waved and started tying her long hair into a pony tail, ready to hit the water.

Nalu jogged up and leaned his surfboard against a palm tree. He turned to look down at Sam, resting his hands on his hips. To Big B, Nalu resembled the palm tree towering behind him. Matted locks of orange hair stuck out in all directions like palm fronds. His eyes were hidden behind reflective sunglasses with black rims. His smile was so big and bright against his brown skin that Big B couldn't help smiling himself.

"Hey, Sam, I see you've found yourself a haole." Nalu spoke to Sam as if Big B were not there.

Sam smiled and offered Nalu a macadamia-nut muffin. "Yeah. Big B, this is Nalu. Nalu, Big B."

The haole and the surfer nodded at each other.

"Are you guys coming in?" asked Nalu.

"He doesn't have a board."

"Well let's at least go for a welcome swim. Come on, we'll swim out to the rocks.

Big B looked at the breaking waves. He was tempted, but all that water made him uneasy. "Uh, you two go. Let me digest this spiru-nut-egg mass in my stomach first."

"Suit yourself, Haole. Come on, Poni."

Nalu and Sam raced out into the blue. .

Big B walked out into the water to get a better look at Sam and Nalu as they dove through the waves, splashing and having fun as they swam to the dark rocks. Rainbow-colored fish darted about in the water. He felt some rubbing against his legs, tickling his skin.

"What is it with fish and me?" He laughed as he looked down, but stopped abruptly, freezing where he stood. Black and white bands swirled and twirled around his legs. Big B stared, petrified. A sea snake was wrapped loosely around his legs, surveying the surrounding water. With each passing wave, the snake gripped slightly tighter, holding itself in place. All the fish had fled. Big B slowly took a deep breath and tried not to make a sound. The snake poked its head out of the water and looked up at Big B. It flicked its tongue in and out. *Can it smell fear?* Big B remained motionless for what seemed like an eternity, watching the snake explore the ocean down around his legs.

Big B remembered that even though sea snakes are deadly poisonous, they were not aggressive. He had seen TV shows with people picking them up. Big B wasn't going to move and he certainly wasn't going to pick it up. His fear started to wane as he realized that the snake appeared oblivious to him, like his legs were just two ordinary trees jutting up from the sand. Satisfied that there was nothing to eat nearby, the snake unwrapped itself from his legs and slipped off into the sea. As the sound of his own heartbeat quieted in his ears, Big B flicked his tongue at his new poisonous friend and backed up to dry land.

Big B headed up the beach and lay back on his elbows, watching Sam and Nalu playing and laughing out in the water. He admired the beautiful cove. *Jack would love this place*, he thought as he watched the breeze swaying the palm fronds above him. He noticed a cluster of big green spheres that hung below the leaves.

The coconuts gave Big B an idea. He grabbed the trunk of the slender palm and shook it vigorously. Nothing happened. He could barely move the tree. He took a few steps back to get a better view of the challenge above him and tripped over a big green nut sitting in the sand. He looked around until he spotted a big lava rock a few steps away. As if it were a football, he launched the nut at the rock. With a smack, it bounced off right back at him. He tried to dodge it, but it smacked him in his knee.

"Ow!" he hollered, hopping up and down, holding his leg.

Furious, he grabbed the coconut and smashed it on that same rock firmly with two hands. The green outer layer broke open revealing brown fibers within. Big B was puzzled. He peeled at the wound he'd made, uncovering more fibers. After smacking and peeling away several more inches of the tightly woven fibers, he finally held the hard brown interior nut.

Big B smacked it onto the rock. With a loud crack, it broke in two. Milk spilled onto the sand and vanished, leaving nothing but a dark wet stain. Big B brought the halves up to his face. He tipped one and got only one drop of milk that he shook off the jagged edge of the shell. From the other half, he got nothing.

He growled in frustration and threw the halves into the bushes. Then he remembered what his football coach told him to do when he was frustrated. He took a deep breath and focused his mind on the goal. He kicked around the edges of the bushes, searching for another coconut. He did discover something—something sharp—when his big toe kicked a pointy sharp rock.

"Ow, ow, ow!" He shouted. A tiny hole in his toe dripped blood. He picked up the rock, scowled at it, and then smiled, focusing again on his goal.

He peeled another coconut and inspected the tough interior nut for the best point of entry. He scraped and twisted the pointed rock into the nut and drilled away small bits until he managed to break through the coconut's seemingly impenetrable shell, exposing its milk without spilling a single drop.

He rested the opened coconut in the sand, feeling victorious. With a thump, another nut fell from the tree he could not conquer earlier. Big B repeated his strategy, but this time it only took him half the time. He smiled with pride.

Nalu and Sam emerged from the water. Big B could hear Sam taunt Nalu. "Ha! I won again. You'd better work on *your* technique, *Wanana*, or every girl on this island will be able to swim faster than you." Nalu pulled Sam's ponytail, and Sam pushed him away.

"Girls rule, boys drool!"

"Here," interrupted Big B, holding out the coconuts, "thought you guys might want a little refreshment after your workout." Nalu looked at Sam, then back at Big B, and beamed, his happy cheeks pushing his sunglasses up higher.

"Looks like the haole here has a bit of island in him after all," said Nalu, reaching out for the coconut. "Most tourists try to smash these open and end up spilling all the milk." Big B quietly kicked a little sand behind him, covering up the wet spot left by the spilled coconut milk.

"*Mahalo, E ka Hoaaloha!*" Nalu tilted back his head and drained the coconut milk into his mouth. He laughed and ripped a loud coconut belch that echoed over the sand. "Thanks!"

It feels great to hang with a guy again, thought Big B.

Sam sat on her towel, held up her coconut in a silent toast, and sipped the milk. Nalu disappeared behind a tree and reemerged with an instrument in his hand, a small guitar decorated with intricate zigzags and swirls. He leaned against the palm's trunk.

Before he started to play, he lifted a white conical shell that was dangling from a string around his neck up to his lips. He whistled a happy, uplifting sound through the shell.

"Now you'll see why we call him 'Wanana.'"

"What's that mean?"

"It means something like 'sixth sense,' which is a special way to connect or to understand. Just watch."

As he played, a crab crawled out of a hole and walked toward Nalu. A butterfly fluttered in and sat on his big toe. A little blue bird circled down out of a palm tree and sat on a coconut shell right next to him.

"That is *so* cool!" Big B laughed. "I wish I could do that for my friends from back home. Boy, I wish *they* were here!"

Big B suddenly realized that might sound rude. He looked at Nalu and Sam, a little ashamed.

"Hey, it's worth a try," Nalu picked up a much bigger shell within arm's reach and chipped off the tip of the pointy end by banging it on a rock. He smoothed it on the rough volcanic stone. He blew off a little shell dust and held it to his lips.

"Uuuuueeeee," Nalu blasted out a sound that started deep and low and ended high and clear.

"Hey, that sounds like 'Nui,'" laughed Big B.

Nalu nodded. "I guess it does."

"I've been wondering. What does *Nui* mean?"

"'Big, abundant, or important.'" Nalu handed the shell to Big B, who studied it for a moment then placed his lips over the opening. He blew as hard as he could but no sound came out other than a pathetic-sounding, scratchy wisp.

"Not very big," giggled Sam. Nalu laughed and picked up his guitar.

"Now check this one out, Nui B."

Nalu played an upbeat island tune. Big B rested back on his elbows, enjoying the unexpected performance. As Nalu played, his audience grew. More small creatures emerged from the bushes and seemed to listen, entranced by his melody. A sea turtle swam into the cove, raising its beak-like head out of the water. A dolphin suddenly surfaced with a chattering sound coming from its smiling mouth, as if singing to Nalu's tune.

"The Wanana plays for his people," Sam whispered. Big B watched the performance in amazement. Nalu captured the attention and trust of every animal in earshot. "He who talks with nature."

Something prickled Big B's leg. He froze, thinking of the snake, but when he looked down, he saw a small, green gecko perched on his leg. It climbed to the edge of his knee and moved its head side to side with the beat of Nalu's concert.

"Hey there, Big B. Mo'o thinks you're all right. Any friend of his is a friend of mine." Nalu stopped strumming and rested his guitar against the tree. The gecko scurried off Big B's leg and back into his bushy home. As the animals slipped away, Big B, Sam, and Nalu sat quietly, enjoying the beautiful day.

Suddenly a raucous cawing destroyed the peaceful silence. A seagull dove from the palm branches above them. It swept toward Sam first, buffeting her head with its enormous wings. Nalu tried to grab it, but it dodged away into the air, staying just out of reach. It whipped around, turning on Big B.

Big B felt frightened as the seagull arrowed toward him. *It's the same bird!* he thought as he raised his arms to ward off the attack. The bird fluttered in the air, poking its head between his arms, jabbing at his chest with its open beak.

Again, Nalu came to the rescue, shouting at the bird in his native language. He grabbed his shell whistle and blew a long, loud piercing note. The seagull screeched and wheeled away from Big B. It climbed rapidly into the sky, let out one more cry, and flew out to sea.

Chapter 11

Professor Prune's Study

What was wrong with that seagull?" Nalu asked. "I've never seen that happen before."

"I don't know," said Sam, clearly shaken, "but that was the second seagull attack we've had in the last few days."

"Really? That's strange."

Big B didn't know what to say. He was sure it was the same bird, but he didn't want to sound paranoid. *Oh yeah,* he thought, *the haole thinks he's being stalked by a rabid seagull.* And there was something else bothering him: He thought the bird was trying to get his pendant. Why else would it be jabbing at his chest? He looked down and saw a half dozen red marks where the bird's beak had gotten him—all around where his pendant hung.

"Are you okay, Big B?" Sam asked, her voice full of concern.

"Yeah, I'm fine . . . just surprised. Um, could we head back to the house?"

"Yeah, that's a good idea," agreed Sam. "It'll be time for dinner soon."

The three of them walked back up the steep path toward the farm. When they got to the top of the cliff above the beach, Nalu handed Big B the big conch shell as he said good-bye.

"Hey. If you want to hook up again just blow this and I'll come meet you at the cove. You know, call me on your shell phone!" He busted up at his own joke as he headed for his home. Big B and Sam waved good-bye and continued up the path in silence.

"Do you still want to check out the Professor's study tonight?" Sam asked cautiously.

"Yeah, sure. I mean . . . we have to, right? We have to find out what happened to him." Big B felt less sure than he sounded.

Dinner that night was quiet. Big B thought his grandpa seemed even more subdued, and his mom was clearly worried. As was becoming the pattern, Big B and Sam helped clear the table and then went outside to check out the stars while her parents finished up. A thick fog had begun to roll in, blocking their view, so they walked into the garden. Almost immediately a dark creature dive-bombed Big B. He ducked, covering his head.

"Aahhh! It's back!"

"It's not a seagull. Don't be scared."

"I'm not! What was it?"

"Just a flying fox," laughed Sam, not bothered in the least.

"You've got to be kidding me. Foxes that fly! What's up with this island?" Big B ducked again, avoiding another attack.

"Actually, they're bats," Sam explained. "We have two types of bats on Nui Island. My dad set up a bat house for the flying foxes out there. See?"

"Why?" Big B squinted to see a rectangular silhouette on top of a tall pole in the distance. "I thought they were dangerous." Big B flinched from another flyby.

"You and a lot of other people. Flying foxes are harmless fruit bats—just really big ones. They eat fruit, not people. The little bats, the cave bats, eat tons of insects. We couldn't live on the island without them, let alone grow crops."

"You're kidding. How is that?"

"The fruit bats help by spreading and replanting the fruit seeds, by eating and pooping them out. That makes the planting work easier for my dad. They also pollinate the flowers, just like bees, but at night. And the cave bats, the ones who eat bugs, are a natural pesticide. There are about ten thousand that come out from caves near the beach each night. They eat the insects that eat plants in the garden. And one of those cave bats can eat up to three thousand mosquitoes in a single night! They help us keep the farm in balance."

Big B ducked, this time to avoid two small bats, stumbled back, and landed on his behind in the soft grass. Sam laughed. "Looks like *your* balance could use a little help!"

"Those little ones are fast!" Big B looked up warily before standing. Numbers whizzed through Big B's mind: ten thousand bats eating three thousand mosquitoes in a night. "That's like, wow, thirty million mosquitoes eaten in a single night."

"Yeah, the island would be whole lot itchier without bats."

Sam's parents emerged from the house. "It's time to go, Sam," said Rosa.

"Can I stay a while longer, Mom? I'm teaching Big B about the bats."

"Okay, but not too late. And keep it quiet. Angela and the Professor have gone to bed."

"Okay," said Sam. She and Big B watched her parents walk down the path. As soon as they were out of sight, Sam pulled a small key from her pocket and held it up for Big B to see. "It's my dad's key."

"You *stole* it?"

"I *borrowed* it. Now, come on—and don't make one little sound! We don't want to wake up your mom."

They took off their shoes and tiptoed through the house, and then down the hallway to Professor Prune's locked study. All of a sudden, from outside the house, they heard a shrill cry. Big B's necklace suddenly felt icy cold and Sam's amulet began to glow a deep blue. Big B's heart seemed to stop as he watched the silhouette of a person appear in the glass door at the end of the hallway.

Big B nudged Sam. She squinted, trying to see the person's face. She fumbled and turned on her flashlight, pointing it at the window, but the figure disappeared into beads of water that streamed down the glass. A light rain pattered against the window.

"Did you see that?" asked Sam, grabbing on to Big B's arm.

"Yeah."

"What was it?"

"Just water and my reflection . . . I think." Big B grabbed the light, opened the door, and looked out into the misty rain. There was nothing but grey misty fog.

Big B looked down at Sam's hand, which she still held tightly around his arm. She quickly let go, and, a little embarrassed, began fumbling with the key to the office. The blue light from Sam's stone faded as she unlocked the door to Professor Prune's study. They heard a faint click as Sam turned the knob. The door slowly creaked open. Big B glanced down the hall at his mom's room and was relieved to see that her light was still off.

Sam nudged the study door open wider and motioned for Big B to follow. She slipped gracefully into the dark room. He looked back at the hall window, into the eyes of his own reflection. He scowled at himself with a tough confidence. His red, pointed hair made him look fearless, as if *he* were a pirate. The shiny cylinder around his neck caught a sliver of moonlight beaming in from the window. Quickly, he slipped into the dark study behind Sam. He gently closed the door behind him with a soft click.

They stood together in complete blackness for four loud ticks of the clock. The room smelled like wood, leather, and time. Suddenly, Sam's mini-flashlight illuminated the forbidden room. In the center was a huge wooden desk. The thick legs were carved like mini totem poles, with faces of animals and people stacked upon each other, supporting a heavy wooden slab top. A high-backed leather chair stood behind the monstrous desk. The leather looked worn, like that of an old broken-in saddle. Across from the desk hung an ornate clock, the source of the ticking. Its wooden casing was carved into branches with leaves and flowers, and two wooden pinecone pendulums hung beneath, each from its own chain. The white metal hands pointed to 9:25.

There were also books—books, books, and more books. Floor to ceiling bookshelves on three of the walls held hundreds of books and journals. Sam scanned the room with her flashlight, and then moved closer to one of the shelves so she could read the books' spines.

Big B read the titles of the books over her shoulder, barely able to make out their titles in the dim light. "*A User's Manual to Antioxidants, Cultural Anthropology, The World of Ancient Art, Modern Astrophysics . . .*" The books seemed to cover everything Big B could imagine—and some things he probably couldn't. "What are we looking for, anyway?" he asked Sam, trying to keep his voice low.

"I don't know . . . yet," she answered in a hushed voice.

"What do you mean you don't know, *yet?* Either you know or you don't."

"Well, I guess I'm different from you. I get feelings about things, gut reactions. My mom says I'm intuitive."

"Is that code for clueless?" Big B snickered.

"Okay, then, Mr. Smarty Pants. We need to find out where the Professor has been digging and what he might have discovered. Any ideas?"

"Yeah, one. Have you tried asking him? You seem to be able to translate everything he says," responded Big B, confused.

"That's just ordinary stuff. And yes, I have asked him. But whenever I try to talk to him about the Bone Pirates or where he went on his last expedition, he can't answer. He gets really agitated and then seems to slip into confusion again."

At that moment, a small hidden door at the top of the clock opened and a tiny wooden bird popped out and cried, "Cuckoo," as if it were eavesdropping.

Big B noted with satisfaction that Sam seemed startled.

"Who's the pollo now, Grape Ape? It's only telling us that it's 9:30. Relax."

Then Big B remembered something that might be helpful. "Hey, what about the other night at dinner?" he asked. "For a minute, Grandpa was clear as a bell—how come?"

"I'm not sure. That happens now and then. Maybe it was the katuk."

"Well, whatever happened, it was weird."

"I totally agree." Sam, now in the O section, continued to read the titles of the books aloud: "*Studies in Oceanography, Oxygen: The Most Important Molecule, The Omega 3 Solution, Occam's Razor, A Master Manual to Organic Farming . . .*"

Big B turned to look at the titles of the largest books on the Professor's desk *The Science of Leonardo da Vinci, Ancient Egyptian Engineering,* and *The Encyclopedia of Pacific Nautical History.* He noticed a wooden cabinet behind the desk. The inset glass doors revealed more books inside. He pulled on the ornately carved knob, but the cabinet door wouldn't budge. "What's in here?"

"That's where the Professor keeps his notebooks, his journals of all of his ideas, plans, and discoveries."

"It's locked."

"Hmm. We need them. The Professor keeps the key close to him. He never lets anyone see his journals. He says they build upon each other, guiding him to new discoveries, each one revealing more about the last. But I don't think he even knows where he is lately." Sam continued to scan the room.

"Oh, here!" Sam bent down and pulled a box from a very dusty bottom shelf and brought it over to the desk. She set the box down, opened the lid, and shone the light into its depths. It glowed, capturing the light. Sam lifted out a crystal ball.

"No way! Grandpa's got a crystal ball?"

"Shhhh! Maybe we can use it."

"Let me remind you that Grandpa's not dead."

The crystal ball began turning a warm red, rippling and simmering like lava. It magnified the glow from Sam's necklace.

Beep . . . Beep . . . Beep. Big B's cell phone rang, making him jump.

"Huh?" He flipped open the phone and brought it up to his chest to see who was calling. It read *Power Off.*

Then it beeped again. A message. The same distorted picture appeared that he had been receiving for days.

"What the heck is going on with this phone? It's been like this ever since I got to this crazy island."

Sam moved closer to Big B. She saw the same smeared picture. The red glow from her amulet was reflected on the phone's screen. "Yeah, that's weird."

"I think I'm going to have to toss this thing." Big B shook his head.

"Well, don't toss it in our trash here. Recycle it. That annoying thing is full of toxic chemicals and heavy metals." *It's not the only annoying thing,* Big B thought.

As Sam began turning away, she caught a glimpse of something in the corner of her eye.

"Wait." She spun back and looked closely at the mirror-like pendant hanging from Big B's neck, just above the point where he held his phone. She squinted. "No way."

"What? What is it?" he asked.

"I think the dead have found their own way of communicating with you."

Chapter 12

Message from the Beyond

What are you talking about?" Big B took a step back, a little afraid of the triumphant look in Sam's eye.

"I need something to see it better. I need a . . . a magnifying glass. The Professor must have one in here somewhere."

"I have one. He . . . my grandpa sent me one. It was a gift I got before the necklace."

"Are you serious?"

"Hold on, I'll be right back." Big B quietly crept from the room. In less than a minute he slipped back through the study door, clutching the ornate hand guard like he was holding a cutlass. He held up the magnifying glass in triumph for Sam to see. "It's cool, isn't it?"

"Very. Now take off the pendant and put it on the screen of your phone. Here, let me." Sam set the bottom of the silver cylinder on the screen just below the image. The image on the phone was reflected in the mirrored surface, but instead of a crazy, warped image, the picture in the mirror was now clear. The letters had arranged into a single word. Sam looked at it through the magnifying glass.

"What is it?"

"A message."

"Let me see."

Sam shifted herself and held up the magnifying glass so they could both look through it. "See?"

Big B's eyes widened with amazement. Reflected on the pendant and enlarged by the magnifying glass, he could clearly see a picture of a woman with dark hair, the name "Isabella" floating below her.

"Who's Isabella?" Big B looked at Sam.

Sam stared at the image, a tiny smile pulled at the edges of her mouth.

"Isabella is the name of my grandmother, you know, the first one who was given the Stone of Souls. Mi abuela has come to help us."

Sam looked up at Big B with a hopeful light in her eyes.

"Abuela Isabella, can you help us? Abuela, can you release Professor Prune's spirit from its curse?"

Big B looked at Sam, raising his eyebrows. She took a deep breath and closed her eyes.

Big B interrupted: "Hey, do you think your amulet turns red when your Grandma Isabella is trying to communicate with us? Every time it turns red my phone beeps and we get another message. But I've seen it turn blue, too."

"It used to glow a bright blue after I went surfing or swimming. My mom said it was the spirit of the ocean staying with me. It hasn't been doing that lately. Now it just randomly flickers a pale blue, like it is struggling. It makes me feel a little empty . . . and cold. Even scared. But when it's red, I don't feel that. I feel kind of warm and comforted."

The phone beeped a new message. They peered at the image reflected on the pendant: wavy lines encircling a pile of skulls and bones.

"Is that water around the bones?"

"I don't know," Sam said, chewing her lip as she focused on the image.

"You know, I also keep getting this weird text over and over. ADRIFT HE WENT."

Sam refocused on Big B.

"The weirder part is that the letters always appear out of order first, like this." Big B scratched letters on a piece of paper as he spoke. "F-I-N-D-T, then I think H, but they come in fast, always spelling the same thing."

"Wait a minute." Sam grabbed the pencil and wrote FINDTH. Then above it she wrote ADRIFT HE WENT, crossing out an F, I, N, D, T, and H. "This might be an anagram, a code. You know, a word scramble? The scrambled words hide the real meaning of the code. Let's see if we can find another message using the remaining letters."

"A, R, H, E, W, E, and T"

She reordered the letters. TARWEE. "No." EARWET. "No. Wait. No way!" EWATER. "Look!" Sam held up the paper." It read FIND-THEWATER.

"Find the water?" Big B was skeptical. This could not be happening. They could not be getting messages on his cell phone from Sam's dead grandmother. "This does not make sense."

"We'll figure it out. I'm sure of it."

"It's ridiculous," Big B said, getting angry. "There's no way this is coming from your grandmother. Why would she send us a code? How does she even know what a cell phone is?"

"Not everything in life is logical, Big B," Sam replied, somewhat defensively.

"Well, if your Stone of Souls is telling us something, why don't you let me try wearing it?" he retorted. "It obviously needs my phone to work."

Sam grabbed her necklace protectively.

"So you're saying you believe me?"

"Well—"

A red light flashed from within her clenched hand, and the phone beeped loudly three times. Another warped image appeared. They peered through the magnifying glass at the reflection in Big B's necklace. Big B gasped. It was a little image of a boat. A black boat with "Bloodlust" painted on its side—the same boat he had seen inside the ship's log. DANGER! flashed three times across the bottom of the screen.

"Bloodlust. Adrift he went? The *Bloodlust* is coming!" He could feel goosebumps lifting the hairs on his arms. Sam didn't say anything, but she shivered.

Their unease was intensified by the faint blue light fading in and out from the stone of Sam's necklace.

"Okay. Ummm. I have something to tell you. It didn't make sense to me before. I thought I was seeing something, hallucinating or something."

"What?"

"When we were up on the Vista. I think I saw it. Down in the ocean. Sailing by."

"Saw what?"

"The *Bloodlust*."

Sam stared at him in shock.

She opened her mouth as if she were about to speak, but then her gaze shifted to something behind him and a frightened look came across her face. Big B whipped around. A dense mist was seeping under the door. It slowly began filling the room, casting a blue, watery light upon the walls. As the fog advanced the room grew colder. It swirled around their bare feet, hovered around their legs, and climbed higher, enveloping them up to their neck. They were pinned with fright, frozen like statues. Sam's flashlight began to flicker. She shook it a few times, and then it went out entirely. The glow from Sam's necklace steadily intensified, enveloping the room in an eerie blue. Strangely, the fog suddenly released them and swirled over the Professor's desk. The books flipped open, and their pages tossed back and forth.

All of a sudden Sam's necklace started to float up into the air, pulsing its deep blue. Big B looked down and saw the blue eyes in his necklace were glowing the same color.

Another screech from outside the house interrupted the silence, and both Sam and Big B jumped, startled. The mist swirled up around the cuckoo clock. The clock's wooden bird popped out of hiding, walked its plank, looked down upon Sam and Big B. With a deep English accent it said, "Professor Prune will always be Cuckoo! Cuckoo! Cuckoo! Cuckoo!"

Then, just as suddenly as it started, the haunting stopped. From out of nowhere, a gust of tingling warm wind blew the glowing blue mist under the door, submerging the room in black silence. Sam grabbed Big B's arm. The clock resumed its rhythmic tick, tick, tick, tick.

"What the . . . ?"

Sam gulped and tried the flashlight again. A strong ray of light shot out, emphasizing their shadows on the walls. They stared at each other in fear, until the quiet was stirred by a slight sound coming from the hallway. Sam redirected her flashlight at the doorknob. It was still.

The noise grew clearer, and they realized it was the sound of trickling water. A shadow cast by the moonlight moved under the door.

With hearts pounding, they tiptoed carefully to the door. Every cell in their bodies was clenched with fear. Big B looked at Sam, her wide eyes had filled with terror. He realized that he probably looked the same. He frowned with intensity, summoning his courage. He touched the door-knob. Cold. He slowly turned it. It squeaked just a little. They peered out. The hall was misty and damp, and they could barely see into the mist, even with the light.

They squinted, but no one was there. Big B bravely stepped out into the hallway, but quickly jumped back. His foot had felt something icy cold. Sam pointed the light at the floor and they saw that Big B had stepped into a puddle of water.

Sam swept the beam of light down the hall into the house. Nothing. She shone it in the other direction and the light revealed a rivulet of water, running out of the house, out into the darkness through the half-open garden door, which moaned as it swung gently in the misty breeze.

"Someone . . . or something . . . was here," Sam whispered, shining her light out into the night.

Chapter 13
the mermaid's tale

W hat's going on?" Sam held the flashlight close to her body, so that the light illuminated her face from below, creating a haunting glow. "Wh-what just happened?"

"Somebody's just playing a trick on us . . ." Big B tried to sound casual, fearless. "You should see your *face*! You would make a great jack-o-lantern! Actually, you look more like a *scared*-o-lantern," he laughed nervously, giving her a little push the way he used to do with Jack.

"Back off!" Sam shone the flashlight into Big B's eyes.

"Sorry." Big B placed his hand over the end of the flashlight, blocking its glare. His fingers turned red, capturing the light within his hand. "Let's call it a night, okay?"

Sam looked at the door, but didn't respond. It occurred to Big B that Sam had to walk outside to get to her house, down the road, in the dark, alone.

"Hey," he said, suddenly sounding very chipper, "I want to check out those bats some more. You want to show me where you live?"

Without hesitating, Sam replied, "Okay, yeah . . . come on." She turned but then stopped abruptly by the puddle.

"Shoes."

"Right." After they put their shoes back on they gingerly stepped around the glistening puddle and walked out the door, through the garden and past the boxes of compost.

As they walked, Sam pointed out the bat houses, explained how her dad had built them, described how the bats used them to sleep and raise their young. She said anything she could think of to prevent silence or a discussion of what had just happened in the study.

"Look, my house is just up there." Sam pointed to lights a short distance ahead. "Here, catch. You'll need this." She tossed the flashlight to Big B. A cave bat dodged around the flying flashlight, right at the last second, and went in search of a better insect.

"You'd better go try and get some sleep. We've got a lot to figure out tomorrow!" Sam turned and sprinted toward her house. Her purple hair caught the light from its windows. It danced from side to side as she ran up the stairs to her porch. With a quick wave, she was gone.

Big B was alone in the garden with the hungry bats, a dimming flashlight, and who knew what else. He turned and sprinted back to the main house, high-stepping around the puddles and making sure to close the garden door, and then headed into the bathroom to get ready for bed.

As he brushed his teeth, Big B watched the pendant bounce gently on his chest. He thought about how cool it was to have a pendant that actually decoded secret messages. But thinking about the pendant and the messages quickly led to him to think about the creepy voice from the cuckoo clock.

He turned out the bathroom light and tiptoed across the hallway. The wooden clock in the study called, "Cuckoo" eleven times. He shuddered and rushed into his room, shut the door, and firmly turned the lock. He crawled into bed and switched off the lamp. Pulling up the covers, he finally relaxed, feeling safe.

As soon as he closed his eyes, he drifted into a hazy dream. He was on a beach. The sun was warm and sparkled off the clear waves. Sam appeared in a thick cover of mist. She talked to him, but no words came from her mouth. Instead, strange images poured out from her lips. Twisted random letters, colors, and shapes. Her hair whipped in the wind, first purple, then blue, and finally turning into water, transparent and rippling in the air. Little dolphins swam through the waves of her hair.

The sky turned dark. Sam's face transformed into the shape of her skull underneath, and then the bones darkened to a deep black. Her hair stopped rippling. The dolphins stopped swimming, their little bodies morphed into little dolphin skeletons, and one by one they fell away. The face moved closer to Big B, slowly rising and falling. He stepped back, but it kept coming, closer and closer. With a whisper of passing fog, the face transformed again into Sam's face, but remained black. It dripped with water and seaweed.

Out of the fog, Big B realized he was looking up into the eyes of a wooden figurehead mounted on the bow of a ship—a black ship. It was a carved figure of a mermaid, with Sam's face, its entire body covered in dripping sea slime. Sam's wooden lips whispered, "The Bloodlussst isss coming!"

Big B backed up and bumped into something. It was one of the worm boxes in the yard. He scrambled over the box to avoid a collision with the huge looming ship. With a crunch and a wailing scream, the ship smashed into the worm box, breaking it open. Through the big gash in the box, gold coins poured out onto the lawn. Worms made of golden chains wiggled around. The wooden mermaid then held out a book to him. It was the *Bloodlust*'s ship log. She threw the book to him, but it passed right between his hands like his worst fear on the football field, a total bomb. The book struck him right between his eyes and he fell back into the wriggling gold.

Big B was jolted awake. He rubbed his eyes, switched on the light, and looked around.

"Man, things just keep getting weirder," he muttered.

Awake, he unzipped his suitcase and pulled out the ship's log. He needed to see the page with the galleon illustration. There it was. The *Bloodlust*, including the figurehead of the mermaid from his dream.

He flipped through more pages, studying it with a new intensity. He turned page after page, reading descriptions of days at sea and notes on ships Sneath had attacked, what booty he had captured, and even sketches of fish, plants, and insects that he encountered. Big B knew that somewhere, disguised in the ship's log, were the clues that would lead to Sneath's undiscovered gold and the secret to breaking the curse—if Big B could just find them. He then remembered what his grandpa had told Sam about Ratbeard's last entry. He turned to the last written page in the log, and read the morbid words.

On this day, 29 of May
I choose my place of rest
I see the past, and soon the future
May my bones be blessed!
Death, come! Row thy boat
My shore, your daunting quest
Take my spirit, but leave my curse
To unworthy thieving guests.

Exodus 7:19—21

Big B knew vaguely of Exodus from Sunday school. But he couldn't remember what it was all about. He'd have to look it up.

On the other side of the page was a big smudge of ink. *Maybe water damage?* he wondered. But then it struck him. It looked very similar to the images Isabella had sent to his cell phone. Was that why she had sent him the codes? To help him learn how to solve Ratbeard's encrypted clues? His hand shook slightly as he took off his necklace and set the bottom of the pendant on the page, just below the sketch. He fetched his magnifying glass and looked through at the reflected image.

"What is that?"

He wanted to show the image to Sam, but of course, since it was the middle of the night, he couldn't. He grabbed his cell phone and juggled the book, the pendant, and the magnifying glass until he found a way to balance all three and take a picture. He finally captured the picture, set the objects down, and looked intently at the image framed in an arch.

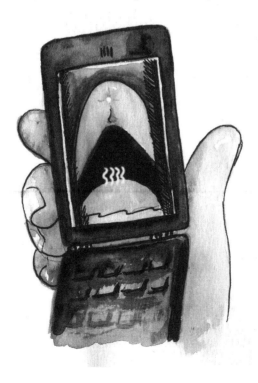

After pressing "Save," he flipped his phone shut and set it back on the desk. Then he noticed that the Exodus verse wasn't the last page of the log. The last page had been torn out. Big B sat staring at the remaining jagged edge. *Now what?* He returned to the sketch of the *Bloodlust* at the beginning of the ship's log.

Speaking to the mermaid's hand-drawn face, he said defiantly, "I'm gonna find that treasure, and I'm going to save my grandpa."

He closed the ship's log with a satisfying smack and slipped it under his bed. He took his iPod out of his backpack, plugged in the earphones, lay back, and stared at the ceiling while Bent Lizard wailed in his ears.

Chapter 14
A Wave of Fear

Big B awoke to the tinkling tune of the wind chime. A gentle breeze blew through his window. He could tell that the sun had already climbed halfway into the sky. He had slept late and was still groggy from his late-night exploration of the ship's log. His earplugs hung from his ears, silent. His iPod battery must have run out during the night. He remembered his dream, the dream of the mermaid, the *Bloodlust*.

Maybe it's time to see if I can find Ratbeard myself, he thought as he pulled on a pair of swim trunks.

He opened the door into the hallway and found himself face-to-face with Sam. He took a quick step back. She was back to her old purple self. No wooden lips, no dripping slime, and no creepy message.

"I thought you would never wake up."

She looked at his swim trunks. "Looks like you have the same idea I do. Come on, let's hit the beach!"

"Well, the beach is always fun," he said, drowsily.

"Gallo, wake up. Nalu's waiting for us. It's time you got in the water."

"Okay, okay, let me get my stuff." He turned back to his room and quickly dropped his cell phone, towel, and the skull pendant into his backpack. *Time you got in the water, ha. My drill sergeant. As if we didn't have anything else to do.*

Rejoining Sam on the porch, he asked, "What about breakfast?" He was starving—it had been a very busy night, with that mermaid dream.

She tossed him a muffin and two bananas. "We'll eat on the way." On the path toward the beach, he turned, looking up at the bat house while jogging backwards.

"Morning, boys!" Big B yelled up to the sleeping fruit bats. "It's a beautiful day!" Sam picked up the pace, her backpack bouncing as she hustled down the beach path.

"What's the rush?" he called, feeling his pulse quicken.

"Surf's up!" Sam yelled back as she wound her way down the hillside switchbacks.

Big B, trying to keep up with Sam, now understood what it meant to eat on the run.

Sam reached a small shed that marked the end of the path to the beach. She disappeared inside and emerged with a surfboard that was, of course, purple. A circular symbol decorated the front end: three swirls formed together in a spiral.

"Cool board."

"Thanks. Maybe I'll let you take her out for a ride. Maybe."

"Her?" he asked, wrinkling his nose and raising an eyebrow.

"Of course, her. All seaworthy vessels are considered female," Sam answered in a condescending tone.

Big B thought about the *Bloodlust* being a girl, a nasty-looking girl . . .

When they reached the beach, Nalu was already there, preparing his board.

"So, haole, you ready to *he'e nalu*? Ready to surf?" Nalu asked.

Big B tried to act relaxed, pretending not to be intimidated by the waves crashing on the reef. "I think I'm going to finish my breakfast first. Why don't you two warm up the surfboards?"

"Suit yourself, Banana Boy. Come on, Sam, let's show him how it's done." Nalu trotted back to the water with his board. Sam took off her necklace and slipped it into her open backpack.

Carrying her purple board, she followed Nalu down the beach to the water. Looking back, she caught Big B's eye and mouthed the word *pollo*, but her look was friendly. Since their visit to his grandfather's study they seemed to be on more level ground.

That was a nice thought, but it faded when he thought of his dream, of Sam speaking but no sound coming out.

He watched Sam and Nalu paddle out on their boards. They bobbed over waves until they were out far enough to sit on their boards. They talked while they floated, waiting for the next set of waves. Big B saw Nalu nod to Sam, offering her the first wave. Sam responded by lying on her belly and paddling into position. The energy of the wave grew stronger, pulling back and arching into a wall of water. Sam paddled madly and got caught in its pull. As the board began to move forward with the wave, she pushed her body up, and then slid her feet under her as the board dropped down the face.

Like a rodeo champ riding a charging bull, Sam rode the wave, channeling its power. She pivoted and turned, cutting into the face of the wave. Her fingers caught the water of the pitching lip, leaving a linear trail of water behind her like a shooting star. Big B was impressed. *She's awesome*, he thought.

As Sam's ride ended in a burst of foaming froth, Nalu's wave beckoned. Nalu paddled calmly out into position. His muscles flexed as he pushed the water behind him. The wave was much larger than Sam's. Nalu paddled hard before getting swallowed by its curl and disappeared entirely behind a curtain of blue, turning water. Just as Big B assumed Nalu had wiped out, an orange crest of hair exploded out from the tube. A blast of spraying water shot out behind him as though he had been shot from a water cannon. He sliced horizontally across the wave and then climbed with increasing momentum. He drove fast down the line, and then launched off the face, back-flipping into the trough behind the foam.

"Sweet!" Big B shouted.

Sam and Nalu each caught more waves before Sam came running out of the foaming surf carrying her board under her arm. "Your turn!"

"Okay." *This is going to be okay*, he thought. *I don't know why I think so, but I do.*

"Be good to her and she'll be good to you," Sam advised, handing Big B her purple surfboard.

"Yes, ma'am." Big B saluted and turned toward the water.

"Good luck!" Sam yelled. "And don't worry, everybody bombs their first day!"

Big B chose to ignore her last comment as he met Nalu at the water's edge.

"Have you ever surfed before?" asked Nalu over his shoulder, paddling out.

"No, but I skateboard a lot."

A small wave broke over his face as he tried to keep up with Nalu.

"No worries, then. You should be a natural." Nalu smiled. "Start small. Get a feel for the wave. Let it start to pull you and invite you to ride it. Once you feel it pushing you forward, plant your feet under you and stand up. From then on it's gonna be like skateboarding on water."

"Cool." Big B nodded, taking in the advice. He followed Nalu out through the waves.

"As we're paddling out, be sure to point your board into the waves. If one is going to break on you, let the wave pass over you. Or you can try going over the top, but be careful. If it catches you, you'll get worked."

Big B decided to power down under the waves. He held his breath, gripped his board tightly, and was consumed by the swell. Under the water, he opened his eyes and saw the beautiful symmetry of the curling wave, passing just above him. As the circular precision spun into chaos overhead, he wondered what it must look like from above.

He felt the power of the crash behind him as he popped out of the back of the wave. When diving under the next wave, Big B looked below him. The water was crystal clear. He caught a quick glimpse of what had to have been hundreds, maybe thousands of fish swimming below, in every color of the rainbow. When he could hold his breath no longer, he popped up again behind a wave to find Nalu sitting on his board, greeting him with a wide white grin.

"Nice job. Most people get worked at least once on the way out. You might do okay out here. Catch your breath for a sec."

Big B bobbed, sitting on his board next to Nalu, who was quiet, staring out at the wide ocean. Big B felt that it was a moment he would never ever forget, for the rest of his life—a magical, life-changing moment.

He looked at the blue water rising and falling around him. Shorebirds flew overhead. He looked back at the beach and saw Sam watching them. Nalu splashed him.

"All right, Big B, this one's yours," Nalu nodded to an approaching swell. "Paddle out, turn, and wait for the wave to just start pulling you in, then paddle hard and catch its momentum."

"Got it!"

His heart thumped against the sticky wax on Sam's board. He paddled into place just as he had watched Sam and Nalu do, and waited. His heart beat harder in anticipation. Suddenly, he was pulled backward, like he was being sucked into a vacuum cleaner. He was looking down as the wave lifted him up from behind, feet first.

Nalu yelled, "Now! Paddle hard!"

Big B dug his hands into the water faster and faster, to move with the wave. He could feel the muscles in his arms tightening with each powerful stroke in the liquid below him. The wave began to push him forward.

Nalu yelled again, "Stand up!"

Big B's heart nervously pounded with the power enveloping his body, and his attempt to push up directly to his feet stopped halfway. He wobbled with one knee resting on the board. In a flash, his mistake in form took its toll. Big B tumbled off his board just as he took a big breath of fearful air. Instantly the ocean grabbed him and swirling, gurgling, bubbling water tossed his body up, down, and all around. He imagined it was what it must feel like on the inside of a washing machine.

As soon as it happened, the chaos of the crash was over, and he found himself on the surface, one hand on the solid form of his board. *Well, it wasn't as bad as I thought it would be,* he thought, catching his breath and coughing a little salt water out of his system. He looked up to see another wave rolling toward him. *I'm not gonna get any better just lying here.* The fear of uncertain consequences now gone from his mind, Big B spat, smiled, turned, and started paddling.

He wiped out again. And again. And again. After a half-hour of crashing, he was exhausted, sore, frustrated, and just about ready to give up.

Nalu paddled up to him, "That was a good one."

"You mean a good wipeout?"

"No, you did much better that time. You were standing for a few seconds before you lost it."

"Yeah, I guess . . ." Nalu's words of encouragement made him feel much better.

"Are you ready to go in?" asked Nalu.

Big B considered it. He really wanted to make it all the way in at least once before quitting for the day. "I'm gonna try one more time."

"Okay, then let's go before this set dies."

Again, Big B paddled forward, turned into position, and felt the now familiar pull. He readied himself as the force of the wave began pushing him forward, faster and faster. He popped up in one motion with a powerful push upward and a solid, balanced stance. The wind blew against his face, and he felt like he was flying. He was surfing! He rode for a blissful minute, and then hopped off his board into the white churn. He looked back at Nalu and raised a fist into the air.

"Yesss!" he exclaimed, dripping with pride.

Nalu hooted back, "Woooo! Way to go, Haole!"

Big B paddled back out. He rode a few more waves, getting more comfortable in the ocean water, feeling the adrenaline rush tingling in his body. The next set was building farther out. He paddled hard to push his board into position farther from land than he'd yet been. Nalu paddled out next to him, smiling ear to ear.

"Going big, Haole!"

Big B looked around. He could see way down the coast where rocky cliffs separated a series of sandy coves. The sun's reflection off the water made him squint, but he could still make out a huge arch that looked as if it had been sculpted by giants.

"Hey, what's that? That arch?" he asked, perplexed. It somehow looked familiar.

"Ah, Pukaaniani, the Window. Legend says that Magma made it to frame the ocean for her youngest daughter's view. Makemake is the daughter, the volcano. But from my perspective, I think it frames the beauty of Makemake herself, reminding me to dream big. There's a good break down there."

Just as Big B was about to ask more about the awe-inspiring formation, Nalu splashed him.

"I'll show you sometime, if you make this wave. Go big, Haole!"

Big B paddled out. He shivered as a breeze blew against his wet back. Suddenly, the wind whistled in his ear, and then seemed to whisper . . . "Bloodlussssst."

He whipped his head around, searching for the source of the sound. He took a breath and tried to calm down. It was just the wind. *Dude, stop freaking out.*

The wave was approaching, so he turned to wait for it to build. Before he could blink, the massive swell pulled him backward. He tried to escape, paddling hard, and then harder. He dug deep, scratching at the water. The wave lifted him up swiftly, and in an instant he realized it was much larger than what he had ridden before. He tried to plant his feet securely, but the wave brutally shoved him off his board. The board dropped through the air and Big B plummeted headfirst into the water, his face slapping the surface. The water seemed harder than asphalt. He processed the pain for only a fraction of a second before the massive weight of the pounding wave crashed on top of him. The force drove him down against the sandy bottom, tumbling him round and round again.

Big B held his breath and opened his eyes, looking for the light of the surface, but he was deep under water in a whirlwind of churning sand and bubbles. It was all a confusion of frenetic froth and swirling space. Then, through the milky white turbulence, he saw a ghastly blue face looking back at him.

A man with a scraggly beard reached out toward him. Big B immediately recognized him—he had the same face Big B had seen instead of his own reflection in the pool. The man appeared colorless, blending into the blue of the water. Wisps of cloth floated away from his ornate but worn and tattered coat and calf-length pants. He looked like a glass musketeer trapped inside a fish tank. His hand made contact with Big B's wrist, and then clutched it tightly.

Big B's hand suddenly felt as if it were encased in ice, and the feeling started to spread up his arm and over his shoulder. He tried to pull away, scratching at where the hand should be . . . but he felt nothing. His lungs seemed to be exploding, and, finally, he could hold his breath no longer. Bubbles of precious air escaped from his mouth and rose rapidly through the water. Still, Big B couldn't escape the deathly grasp. He knew he was about to run out of air.

Though he had been panicking a moment ago, an oddly complacent feeling began to creep over him. Tiny air bubbles slipped through his lips, one by one at first and then in a steady stream. The surface no longer seemed important as he started drifting downward.

Suddenly, something big, slippery, and very strong was underneath him. It pushed him up through the water like a torpedo. He broke the surface and instantaneously gasped at the air in desperate relief. Hyperventilating, he filled his lungs with oxygen, his mind now awake and filled with fear.

He turned and looked into the smiling face of his rescuer—a sleek, grey dolphin. Somehow, that instant of dolphin kindness made Big B feel safe and protected, although completely drained of energy.

When Nalu saw Big B pop out of the water, he quickly began swimming over to him, calling out as he did, "Hey man, you okay? That was one gnarly wipe-out!"

Nalu stopped to rub the dolphin's nose. "Nai'a makes a great lifeguard. She likes you, too. See?" Nai'a chattered at Big B and did a flip in the air.

"Thanks, Nai'a, I owe you one, big time," Big B said between coughs and breaths.

"Dude, you look like you've seen a ghost!" said Nalu, looking concerned. "Come on. The best thing to do after you wipe out is get back on your board and try again."

Big B looked at Nalu, but his eye caught movement in the background. In the distance something was gliding behind the cliffs of the farthest cove, near the window-arch of stone. Through the mist thrown off by the waves breaking hard on the rocks, he thought he saw a black flag waving in the wind. Goosebumps crawled across his skin. He breathed harder.

"No thanks, man. I think I'm done for the day." Big B struck out for shore, where Sam had made camp and gone fast asleep.

He dragged Sam's board and his exhausted body across the warm sand and rested the board against a palm tree, trying not to wake Sam. But she stirred as he pulled the skull pendant out of his pack and slipped it on.

"What's going on?" she said, sitting up drowsily.

"I gotta go," he said sharply and started running back toward the path. He called back as he ran, "Catch a couple more for me."

Sam yelled after him, "Wait, we need to talk about last night! What are . . . ?"

"Later!" And then he was out of sight and sound.

Big B raced up the path, hoping he could catch a glimpse of what he suspected was the *Bloodlust*. He slipped and noticed as he picked himself up that he was already bleeding from a couple of scrapes on his leg and arm. He must have literally sanded off his skin while getting manhandled by that wave.

As he ran he remembered the vision of the floating man . . . the pallid apparition that reached for him, beckoning far below the ocean's surface. He instinctively reached for the pendant around his neck. It was cool inside his hand. He could feel the sharp facets of the sapphire eyes.

Reaching a turnout in the path, he stopped and stepped out onto the overlook. The view was magnificent. He could see all of Palekaiko Cove, the cliffs spaced down the coast, the arch of stone, and the vast ocean beyond. Way out on the horizon he saw several smaller islands.

He shaded his eyes from the sun and scanned the water for the black galleon. He saw nothing but a seagull flying past. It screeched, and he watched as the bird disappeared behind the cliffs. *Could that be the same bird?* he wondered. He heard another screech, but this time it floated up from below.

It was Sam—screaming.

Chapter 15
the Missing Amulet

Big B heard Sam scream again, this time closer.

"Thief! Give it baaack!" Her voice carried loud and clear to where Big B was standing. Alarmed, he looked down and saw her purple hair streaming behind her as she sprinted up the path. As she got closer, Big B could see the fierce look in her eyes. "Give it back!" she screamed, glaring at *him*.

"Give what back?" he asked, taking a step backward, confused.

"You know exactly what, you jerk!" Sam was fighting back tears. She blinked and her eyes glistened. Nalu appeared on the path behind Sam.

"What's going on?" he yelled up at them.

"I have no idea," Big B yelled back. "Ask her!" He pointed a finger at Sam.

Nalu caught up to them on the bluff and looked at Sam searchingly. Sam, trembling with rage, ignored him.

Her eyes narrowed, "*Gallo malo!*" she hissed.

"Dude, I think she just called you an 'evil rooster'!" Nalu laughed at first, but was quickly silenced by the fire in Sam's eyes. "Chill, Sam. What's the problem?" Nalu asked calmly, trying to understand what was going on.

"The Stone of Souls, Nalu." Sam brought her hand up to her bare throat. "I took it off before I went surfing and put it in the pocket of my pack so I wouldn't lose it. He must have taken it when I was asleep, or when I was surfing!" Sam's eyes flared with anger.

"No, I didn't! I wouldn't," pleaded Big B.

"Yes, you did, you must have! I knew you'd want to find the treasure for yourself. Without me! You think mi abuela is gonna help you without me? Now that you stole my necklace? No way!"

"Easy," soothed Nalu, touching Sam on the shoulder.

"Don't touch me!" She shrieked and lurched away, turning to run back down to the beach. Big B and Nalu were left staring at each other, blinking in bewilderment.

"I've never seen her so mad!" exclaimed Nalu.

"Whatever. I'm not a thief!"

"You know, she doesn't really trust people who aren't from the island."

"Why?"

"She loves the island, and some of the people and companies that have moved here have done some things that have changed it and have hurt it. She's had some other haole friends who have turned their backs on her when she really needed them."

"Well, I don't know why she's so mad at me. I never betrayed her."

"So, what *was* she talking about?" Nalu probed.

"What do you mean?" Big B rolled a pebble under his shoe and stared off into the distance.

"You know. What she said about the treasure? About her grandmother?"

"Oh, it's nothing."

"Oh, come on, Haole—afraid of your *girlfriend?*" taunted Nalu.

"Shut up! She's not my girlfriend." Big B kicked the pebble off the bluff.

"Sorry, man, I was just teasing! Just tell me what's going on. Maybe I can help." Nalu sounded genuine, but Big B didn't know if he should trust him. Unfortunately, he didn't know who else he *could* talk to.

"You promise not to tell?" Big B looked hesitantly at Nalu.

"Yeah, of course. They don't call me the Wanana for nothing. I'm good at listening to roosters," Nalu said, tilting his head knowingly.

"Okay." Big B decided to fill Nalu in. He turned and looked behind to make sure they were alone. He took a step closer to Nalu and lowered his voice to a whisper. "Sam and I have to find the Bone Pirates."

Nalu looked at Big B for a moment, and then burst out laughing.

"I'm serious!"

Nalu laughed even harder. "That's got to be the funniest thing I've ever heard. You haoles will believe anything! Man, that's just an old island ghost story. My *tutu*—my grandma—used to tell us about the Bone Pirates to scare my cousins and me into bed." Nalu laughed, his eyes twinkling.

Big B looked irritated.

"So . . ." Nalu stopped laughing.

"What?" asked Big B.

"Did you take it? You know, Sam's necklace?" Nalu stared at Big B, waiting to judge his reaction.

"No!" yelled Big B. "Why doesn't anyone trust me!" His voice cracked in frustration.

Nalu shook his head. "Look, I don't want to get caught in the middle here. You two need to talk this out." With a heavy sigh, he turned down the path to look for Sam.

Big B took off up the path toward the main house, sprinting most of the way up the steep hill. His body ached as much as his heart. *I can't believe she thinks I would steal her necklace. I thought she trusted me!* He stopped running and let out a sigh of frustration.

Dropping exhausted onto the porch steps, he felt as defeated now as he had lying on the pavement outside the mall after breaking Rocco's window. He felt as if he were just waiting for the glass to shatter and rain down on him. He pulled himself up to the porch, collapsed on a bench, and took a few moments just to feel sorry for himself. Slumped against the wall of the house, he thought about the necklace and who might have stolen it. *There was no one else on the beach. It wasn't me, and it couldn't have been Nalu, so who was it?*

"Oh no!" he exclaimed, bolting upright in a sudden wave of understanding: *We can't get any more messages from Isabella.*

"How are we going to find the Bone Pirates now?"

Chapter 16
the Key

"irates!"

Professor Prune's yell made Big B jump and whirl around. He hadn't noticed his grandpa lying in a canvas hammock at the far end of the porch. Big B crept toward the hammock and then stopped to watch his grandfather. Professor Prune twitched in his sleep but didn't utter another word.

Big B sat down on a bamboo bench near the hammock, unsure of what to do next. Two big yellow fruits sat next to an assortment of odd objects on a small table next to the bench: A pocket watch, a key, a multi-tool, a couple of toothpicks, and a thick pair of glasses with round lenses. Big B eyed the key, wondering what it unlocked. He realized that, despite his anger, he was hungry, so he borrowed the multi-tool to peel the skin from one of the pear-shape fruits. He sheared off a slab of sweet flesh and carefully bit it off the knife. He stared at the key while he chewed, feeling angrier and angrier by the minute.

"Why doesn't anyone trust me?" Big B wondered aloud. His grandfather breathed in and out rhythmically, deep in sleep. "Mom thinks I'm dangerous, Sam thinks I'm guilty, and Nalu thinks I'm an idiot. This sucks!" he ranted. "I wish we had never come here!"

"Come here . . ." the Professor echoed, rolling over in the hammock. His weight shifted suddenly, flipping the hammock over. It dropped the Professor onto the porch floor with a loud thud.

Big B laughed, but immediately covered his mouth, realizing his grandfather might be hurt. The Professor peered up at him through puckered eyes. His hair stuck out from all sides of his head, making him look like a helpless baby bird.

"Are you okay, Grandpa?" he asked. Professor Prune sat up and stretched up a hand. With Big B's help, his grandfather lifted himself off the floor. He felt on the table for his glasses and put them on. Smoothing down the wispy hair around the base of his bald head, he nodded at Big B.

Big B cut off another chunk of fruit and offered it to his grandfather.

"Here. Looks like you could use a bit of energy."

The Professor grunted, accepting the snack. He swallowed it with one gulp and Big B thought he caught a gleam in his eye. The old man slowly collected his possessions from the table. He returned the watch and toothpicks to one pocket and the key to the other. He looked at the multi-tool in Big B's hand.

"Oh, sorry!" apologized Big B. "I was just borrowing it to peel the fruit, your fruit. You want some more?" His grandfather shook his head.

He felt slightly guilty for using the knife and eating the fruit without asking. He fished his towel out of his backpack, cleaned the juice off the blade, and snapped it closed.

With his towel around his neck, he handed the multi-tool to his grandfather. "It's all clean now, okay?"

Big B watched while the Professor put the multi-tool into the same pocket as the key.

"Glum mith wee," the Professor said, tugging on Big B's arm and leading him toward the porch door.

Big B obediently followed his grandpa outside and across the property, toward a building that Big B had noticed but had not yet explored. The Professor pressed a finger onto a black pad by the door. The door clicked, and he grabbed the handle and pulled. He hesitated, turning toward Big B, putting a finger to his lips.

"Shhhhhh." The unruly white eyebrows lifted in confidence. Big B understood and nodded.

"Plum gin, by moy!" The Professor opened the door wide. He showed Big B in with a sweeping gesture of welcome.

When Big B stepped inside the building, all he saw was a short hallway. But he heard the sounds of bubbling and the hum of machinery. The Professor looked back outside and then closed the door behind them. The hallway led to a large room where Big B saw Armando. Leaning over an experiment in a white lab coat, his face was twisted with concern, puzzling over a problem. He looked up from his work, sensing company.

"Big B!" Armando's face relaxed and lit up. "I see the Professor has brought you to his lab. Quite an honor. He doesn't trust many people with his secrets, you know."

Big B looked over at his grandpa. He was puttering around the lab, peering into test tubes, then into the hollow center of a roll of paper towels. His grandpa looked up and gave him a nod.

Big B smiled. *Maybe someone trusts me after all*, he thought. *Yeah, the someone studying the table through a paper-towel roll microscope.*

"Phew! What's that smell?" Big B asked Armando, wrinkling his nose. "It's like rotten eggs."

"Bacteria, Big B. We've been sampling bacteria from all over the island, from every kind of habitat we can find."

"Why?"

"Do you know much about bacteria?"

"Other than that it can make you sick, not too much. Oh, yeah," suddenly remembering Sam's lesson, "and it can make biogas."

Armando nodded. "Well, only a few kinds of bacteria can make you sick, and only a few make biogas. But there are millions of kinds of bacteria, and they do millions of kinds of things. Bacteria are very old. They were the first life forms to appear on Earth billions of years ago. In all that time living on Earth, they have adapted and created so many ways to make energy, to break down life, recycle it, and create new energy for other living things. They are like little scientists."

"What do you mean?"

Armando walked over to a humming machine and opened the lid. He checked on small vials being picked up and moved around by a small robotic arm.

"Well, they are always experimenting and inventing in their own way. When bacteria evolve to live in a new environment or eat a new food, they create new chemicals and try out new reactions. Their survival depends on having a working solution. Solutions enable them to produce their offspring, and then the next generation and on and on. Only the fittest survive."

"All this time experimenting has enabled bacteria to invent chemicals, biological cycles, and, honestly, ideas that could benefit us. And not just bacteria. We look at all kinds of life forms to get ideas and then try to engineer things that will benefit people."

"Like what?"

Armando noticed the shark tattoo on Big B's arm. "Check this out."

Armando rubbed his hand across a grey square of material lying on the counter. Big B copied him. It felt like sandpaper.

"Rub it in the other direction."

It felt smooth.

"Now look at it magnified a thousand times in the electron microscope."

Armando flipped a switch and a TV screen came to life. The image was filled with hundreds of little three-tipped sharp points with wavy grooves that looked like a cross between very sharp teeth and the snowplows back in Chicago, all arranged tightly together like puzzle pieces.

"What do you think it is?"

"It looks like some nasty armor that a knight would wear."

"Good guess." Armando nodded down at Big B's tattoo. "Shark skin."

"No way! It looks as fierce as a shark."

"Well, it's not its attitude that we are interested in. A shark swims in the same direction that feels smooth to you when you rub your hand across the skin. All those tiny points on his skin reduce friction with water, making him swim faster. Nature has enabled the shark to live in balance with the water around him, to adapt so he interacts with water in a very, shall we say, intelligent way. The Professor has been investigating to see if we can copy the structure of his skin in some way to make ship hulls move through water with less friction, which means using less energy, like the shark does."

"Maybe I can wear a sharkskin swimsuit and be in balance with the water."

"It might be a little stiff, but that's the idea. Maybe we could mimic the microscopic pattern of his skin in a modern fabric, and you could swim as fast as a shark."

"Now you're talking."

"Its called biomimetics. *Bio* for 'life' and *mimetic* for 'mimic.' Biomimetics copies what nature does and tries to apply it to our problems."

Big B smiled a little, thinking of Sam. How she sounded just like her dad.

"Life is beautiful, Big B, and it is full of ideas that could help our planet. The Professor is especially excited about ancient life, the oldest life on earth—bacteria. He thinks they hold keys to solving some of the most important problems for people. Ways to make life better—no, make life amazing. So, I am looking."

"Looking for what?"

"Well, that's the problem. Only the Professor knows. He leaves me a list of things to do in the lab. Lately, though, I think he has forgotten what he is looking for. It all started a few weeks ago when he went out to search for some artifacts or bones, maybe."

"Yeah, Sam told me what happened."

With the mention of bones, Big B heard the sound of water pouring loudly onto the floor. Armando and Big B turned to see the Professor standing next to a low-walled aquarium built on top of a lab bench. He was holding his hand up and blocking a stream of water that had been flowing into the aquarium. Water that was supposed to pour out of a pile of rocks and cascade into the aquarium instead ran down the Professor's arm and spilled onto the lab floor, spreading out into a big puddle.

Armando rushed to his side, Big B right behind him. "Don't worry, Professor, it's just water." Armando tried to pull the old man's arm away, but he resisted.

The Professor looked at them both. "Vater. Doost vater? Vut tay doon bootha trepcious vater?"

"Water? What is he talking about?" Big B asks nervously.

"I don't know, but he has been talking about water since, well, since the day he went looking for—"

"The bones," concluded Big B in a chilling voice.

With the mention of the word *bones* a second time, the Professor pulled his hand back, and looked down at droplets falling from his fingers into the water spreading across the laboratory floor. He wiped his wet hand on Big B's shirt, and patted him gently, looking into his eyes. Big B returned his gaze, seeing his own reflection in his grandfather's glasses.

Armando noticed the dried blood on Big B's leg and arm.

"What happened to you?"

Big B looked down at his scrapes.

"Oh, that. Learned to surf this morning." He slid his hands into the back pockets of his swim trunks. He felt something unexpected in the left pocket. His eyes grew round as he felt the shape of a key. He looked at Grandpa. The Professor was wandering away, mumbling and fidgeting with a petri dish.

"Uh . . . I guess I'd better go back to the house and clean up," Big B said, wanting to check out the key immediately. "Thanks, Armando, for showing me the lab. It's really cool."

Armando smiled. "My pleasure, Big B. Here, take this—wash those scrapes out good with soap. Then mix one part of this with three parts fresh water, and use it to clean around that one bad cut there."

Armando handed Big B a small vial full of a clear gel. "It will help kill off any bad bacteria that could infect your cut. Then put this bandage on and keep it dry for a day, okay?"

"Yeah, sure. What is this?" Big B held the vial up to the light.

"Its active ingredient is made by that living machine over there." Armando pointed to a big glass tube about as tall as Big B, with lots of smaller tubes around it. "It's full of a unique kind of bacteria."

Big B smiled, realizing the odd twist of bacteria creating something to kill other bacteria. He zipped the vial and bandages, along with his towel, into his backpack.

"And do you know what is really cool about this?" Armando put a few drops of the liquid from the machine into a small glass dish and held it up for him to sniff. Big B recognized the smell. Armando stepped back away from him and put on a pair of goggles.

"Do you remember the Cruiser?"

Just as Big B understood what the gel was, Armando dropped a burning match into the dish, and a little puff of fire flashed for a second, then was gone.

"Ethanol!"

"Yes, it's an alcohol that a type of bacteria can make. Very good, Big B. You have science in your blood. Speaking of which, where's Sam?"

"Uh," Big B stopped and looked at the floor. "She's still at the beach," he said, his voice quiet. "I gotta go. Thanks, Armando. Bye, Grandpa."

The Professor was startled from a nap—a nap he had just started while still standing. He grunted and smiled. Big B was sorry that his grandfather seemed so confused, so lost. He turned and hurried out the lab door. Once outside, he pulled the key from his pocket to examine it. It was the same key he had seen on the porch table. The same one he saw his grandpa put in his pocket after his nap. But how did it get into *his* swim trunks?

What does it open? he wondered, studying the key. It was ornate and heavy. It looked as though it would open some type of box or case. Then Big B remembered the locked cabinet in his grandpa's study.

The journals. It must unlock the cabinet where he keeps his journals! Big B looked up and was startled by a face leering back at him. It was the face of the dark grey seagull—the same one that had attacked him twice. He was sure of it.

The seagull sat on a bamboo railing. Dirty and tattered, it stared at him through bright blue eyes. The seagull cocked its head and looked closely at the shiny key. An odor like rotting fishy garbage drifted over to Big B. Hopping closer, the gull hissed and snapped its beak. Big B closed his fist tightly around the key and ran for the house. He could hear the seagull shriek. He looked back and saw it flying after him. The seagull shrieked again, this time even louder. The bird was close, right next to his ear, and he could smell its rotten stench. Big B stepped hard to the right, and then spun backwards to the left. Like his best offensive move, he changed direction again and again, trying to shake the seagull from its pursuit.

Big B rounded the corner of the house and was blinded by the sun. As he raised a hand up to block the sun, his feet rolled out from under him. His hands opened to catch his fall, and like a terrible fumble on the football field, he released the key.

He heard the brass clinking away in front of him as he tumbled to a stop. He lifted his head up to see the key lying on the stone path, just out of his reach.

Then the seagull swooped down from above, screeching.

Chapter 17
the ghost in the glass

t he bird landed next to the key, and cried out in victory, a noise that sounded like laughing. *Ki-yah-yah-yah*! It snapped its beak and poked at the key. Big B scowled in anger. He felt something digging painfully into his wrist; it was one of the nuts that had brought him tumbling to the ground. He slowly moved his hand and grasped the nut tightly in his fingers. The bird picked up the key, flapped its wings, and started to rise. Big B rose, too, tracking the bird.

Like a skilled marksman, Big B whipped the nut toward the foul creature. With a loud clink, the nut struck the key dead on, knocking it out of the startled bird's beak. Big B ran as hard as he could and then dove for the falling key. With the same hand that fumbled earlier, he made a perfect diving catch. Then he leaped up and ran for the house.

Staying only one step ahead of the devilish bird's hot pursuit, he sprinted through the garden, whipped open the glass door, and slid into the hallway. The door slammed behind him, just rescuing him from another aerial attack. Safe!

Panting, Big B stared at the ratty seagull through the glass door. The bird's blue eyes glowered back at him. They seemed to flicker like Sam's amulet. It paced on its webbed feet and pecked viciously at the door. Big B guarded the door patiently, catching his breath.

"Phew! That was close!"

He uncurled his fingers to double-check that he really had rescued the key. The bird cocked its head and stared intently through the glass. Big B quickly closed his hand, retreated to his room, and firmly shut the door. After closing the window and pulling the curtains closed, he stashed the key under his pillow for safekeeping. He returned to the window and peered outside, but the dirty seagull was nowhere in sight.

He pulled out the vial of Armando's cleanser from his pocket and peeked out into the hallway. The bird wasn't by the glass door anymore, either. He walked toward the bathroom, but stopped short, hearing his name. His mom was talking with Rosa in the great room.

"I just didn't know what to do, Rosa. Brett was making the wrong choices back home. He was hanging out with the wrong friends, getting into more and more trouble." He heard his mom sigh. "When you called about my dad, I thought maybe this was exactly what Brett needed. A fresh start."

"You did the right thing, Angela," Rosa assured her. "I think Sam needed a change, too. She has become so involved with her world here on the farm that she hasn't been spending much time with friends her own age. Big B has allowed her a chance to build trust in a real friend, someone besides the katuk and tomatoes. I am glad for this."

"Don't be too glad," sulked Big B, muttering to himself. "Sam doesn't trust me anymore."

He shrugged and headed into the bathroom to clean his scrapes. He turned on the faucet and filled a glass with water, and then added part of the clear antibacterial gel. It swirled into abstract opalescent designs as it sank through the water. Big B held the glass up to the light. He watched the gel slowly morph, suspended by the water. Just as he picked up a swab to dip into the solution, the clear mixture fused into the shape of a face—a familiar face. It was the face from the pool, the face from under the wave—and now it was inside his glass!

In a second, the haunting face disappeared and was replaced by a high-pitched shattering sound. Big B looked down to see shards of the glass lying in the sink. The liquid face slipped through its broken edges, leering up at him as it slithered down the drain.

"Are you okay, honey?"

Startled, he looked up to see his mom standing in the doorway.

"What happened?"

Big B blinked as if waking from a dream. "Uh, I dropped it. I dropped the glass. It slipped."

"Well, let me help you clean it up." She touched his shoulder gently, looking into his face. Big B could tell that she was worried.

"I'm okay," he said, shrugging her off. "Hey mom, I surfed today! Check out my cool sand rash!" He proudly showed off his scrapes and cuts. "Armando gave me this antibacterial gel to clean them up. I guess the glass just slipped out of my fingers." He smiled a sheepish grin.

His mom carefully picked up the pieces of glass and dropped them into the wastebasket. She scanned the floor for any stray shards.

"You boys and your battle wounds! Looks like most of the glass stayed in the sink. I think I got it all, but why don't you sweep the floor just to make sure. First, though, let's go to the kitchen and take care of those scrapes."

He followed his mom into the kitchen and allowed her to clean him up. They used what was left of Armando's disinfectant and applied it to his wounds. She applied then kissed his bandages the way she had when he was four years old, after he tried to ride his bike for the first time without training wheels.

"Thanks, Mom, for the first aid . . . and the *kiss germs*." He squirmed and made a face at her.

"You're welcome," she said.

Big B grabbed the broom and headed back to the bathroom.

"Later," he said.

He swept the bathroom floor and found only a tiny piece of glass, which he carefully put into the wastebasket. The shard reminded him of the glass from Rocco's broken window, glistening on the pavement all around him, and he felt a pang of guilt. He leaned the broom against the door frame and looked into the empty sink. Shaking off a shudder, he stepped across the hall, closed the door to his room, and then sat down on his bed.

Big B pulled out the brass key from under the pillow and studied it in his fingers. He wanted to go home. He thought about Jack and skateboarding at the mall. And he thought about Sam. *What do I do now?*

Staring at the ceiling, turning the key over and over in his fingers, he considered everything that had happened over the last few days: the seagull attacks, the ghostly figure, and the weird events in his grandfather's study.

"Sam has to believe I'm not a thief. I've got to prove it somehow," he muttered. "I've got to look at those journals!"

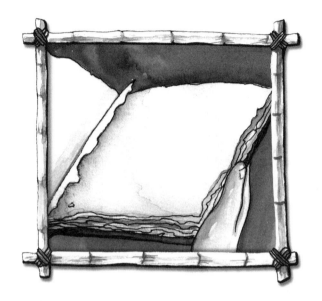

Chapter 18
the missing page

Big B changed out of his swim trunks and into fresh clothes, and then slipped quietly across the hall to the study. The door was locked, and Sam had returned her father's key the night before. How was he going to get inside? He tiptoed down the hall and peered into the kitchen. No one was there. He went over to the screened porch and looked out across the grounds. He saw his mom and Rosa walking away from the house, wearing hiking gear.

That will give me some time, he thought.

He looked for a solution, a way to get into the study. He pulled open some drawers in the kitchen, looking for something that could release the lock. Inside a utility drawer, he found what he was looking for, a pair of thin-bladed scissors. Jack always used a pair of scissors on the lock to his brother's room. Big B hoped these would get him past the study's locked door.

Big B inserted one of the scissors blades into the lock's keyhole and wiggled it. No luck. He tried again, but the lock wouldn't turn. On a whim, he tried the brass key. It slid into the keyhole, but it was too small. Big B was afraid if he turned it too hard the key would break inside the lock. Frustrated, he tried the other blade of the scissors. He inserted it and this time turned forcefully. He heard a loud *snap!* The doorknob turned freely, admitting him into the room. He looked down the hallway, first left, and then right, and then he slipped into the room unseen. The rhythm of the cuckoo clock greeted him—tick-tick-tick-tick—seemingly keeping time with his heart.

He went directly to the locked cabinet and slid the brass key into the lock. It fit perfectly and turned easily. The lock clicked and the door popped open.

Peering into the open cabinet, he thought, *Finding the solution to Grandpa's problem may take a while.* He counted ten books inside, and then began pulling them out one by one. Each one was covered in brown fabric. He read the titles and browsed through the opening pages of each journal, then stacked them in a pile on the floor. Every book title began with *Advances In*, which was then followed by a different topic like *Solar Solutions, Renewable Kinetic Energies,* and *Conservation Reserves.*

Inside each journal were pages and pages of writing, equations, and drawings, all by the same hand. Big B looked more intently at one book. Its subject, *Advances in Water Webs,* was vaguely familiar since his arrival at the farm. It reminded him of the terrifying image of the water-ghost slipping down the drain of the bathroom sink. He opened the journal and began flipping through its pages.

He recognized sketches of things Sam had shown him: The fish ponds, the algae channels, the digester, and the worm boxes were all detailed in the beginning of the journal. Flipping through more pages, he was quickly overwhelmed by the massive amount of information his grandpa had captured in ink.

Further into the water web journal, he saw sketches of the same systems from the farm drawn on a much larger scale, designed to work for the largest city on Nui Island. There were detailed maps of the city and maps and colorful photos taken from satellites of the entire island. Drawings showed ponds, huge algae channels, the domes of biogas digesters, and even giant worm boxes churning out truckloads of black gold.

Big B traced the perimeter of Nui Island on the map with his finger. He followed arrows and lines that linked the pieces of the Professor's wastewater solutions to the bigger island-wide puzzle. He stopped and held the book at arm's length to get a wider perspective.

"Hmm. It does look like a spider web."

Further into the book, he found calculations written over maps of the United States and the world.

"Wow! Grandpa thinks big."

Smack!

Big B jumped, startled by a loud sound from within the book cabinet. He peered in and saw that a book had fallen down and slapped against the wooden shelf. It must have been standing up against the back of the cabinet, hidden behind all the other journals he had taken out. He pulled the book out. "Gray Industries Annual Report" was printed in black on the pale cover. The word CONFIDENTIAL had been stamped in red ink over the title.

Inside were descriptions of more projects on the island—power plants, resort developments, fossil fuel exploration—and more maps and more pictures taken by satellite.

After the images came pages and pages of financial information. Money, money, and more money. He had seen a few annual reports, like this one, from companies his dad was interested in.

Evidently his grandpa was quite interested in *this* company. His writing was all over the report. He had circled things and written comments, including some phrases with lots of exclamation points. Big B saw, more than once, "This must be stopped!" written in red ink in the Professor's handwriting. He wondered what it all meant.

Hoping for some help, he pulled out his cell phone and flipped it open. But no message appeared.

"Right. I don't have the Stone of Souls." He sighed and put his phone away. "I guess I'm on my own."

He skimmed through more of the report. Three-quarters of the way through he came across a yellowed piece of paper that had been folded and tucked between the pages. The heading on the left-hand page read, "Subterranean Water Flows." Grandpa's handwriting was in the margins around the text. Some words were circled with lines connecting them, creating a pattern similar to the Professor's wastewater web drawing. The words "Ma'ema'e Reef" had been written in and then circled several times with red ink.

Big B unfolded the piece of paper. He recognized the handwriting immediately. It was the missing page from Ratbeard's journal!

ONE BY LAND, THREE BY SEA
IN LINE WITH DARK'S BRIGHT STAR
I WILL WAIT FOR THEE
ONE WILL BE, MANY YOU'LL SEE
BUT THE KEY TO MY RICHES
LIES BENEATH ME

Seek Wisely or Dread
You Will Lose Your Head
And Your Thoughts Within Will Flee
For Time You Will Dwell
Sealed Like Pearl In Your Shell
While Spirits In Our Bones Go Free

If Attacked By My Curse
You May Feel Even Worse
To Know I Have Left You The Cure
But This Antidote Creeps
While Your Mind Begs And Weeps
From The Poison That Plagues Your Bright Shore

Big B skimmed the riddle again, and then read aloud phrases that caught his eye. "You will lose your head" *Grandpa didn't seek wisely. He must not have found Ratbeard's bones.* "The key to my riches lies beneath me." *The key to the riches is still out there. And the antidote to Grandpa's illness! But where? I've got to help him! If this riddle led Grandpa to the pirates, it will lead me, too. And to the treasure. I just have to figure out how.*

Big B slipped the paper into his pocket. He gathered the journals and replaced them in the cabinet exactly as he had found them, and then carefully closed the door and locked it securely with a reverse twist of the key. There was a tap when he finished twisting, but not from the lock.

Big B looked slowly around the room trying to find the source. A slight movement in the window caught his eye. The seagull sat on the windowsill, its crooked beak pressed against the window. Big B rushed toward the window and smacked the glass. The bird flew off, flapping its tattered wings and leaving a big black poop on the windowsill.

His heart now beat furiously. Big B quickly slipped out of the study, pulled the door closed behind him, and slid the scissor blade into the lock. In his haste, he twisted the scissors too hard, and the tip of the blade broke off, jammed inside the mechanism. The door, adrift from its broken lock, creaked open a tiny crack.

Chapter 19
Krill

Back in his room, Big B put the key in a small hidden pocket in his backpack and hid the broken scissors in the back of the desk drawer. He glanced out the window and realized that the light was fading. It would soon be time for dinner. Looking around the room, he considered hiding places for the piece of paper he'd taken from his grandfather's study. He finally settled on his suitcase, unzipping it and pulling up a corner of the lining so that he could slip the piece of paper beneath it.

Dinner that night was quiet. Sam wouldn't look at Big B and eventually he stopped trying to capture her attention. At one point, he saw his mom look at Rosa with raised eyebrows. Rosa just shrugged in response. *Well, it's not my fault we're not talking,* he thought. Rosa hadn't commented on the missing necklace, so Sam must not have said anything to her parents . . . yet.

When dinner was over, Rosa came to the rescue. "Big B, why don't you take the night off," she said kindly. "It sounds as though you had a rough day of surfing."

"Yeah . . . thanks." Once he was back in his room, Big B retrieved the slip of paper from his suitcase and pulled out the ship's log from under his bed. He opened the tattered book and held the piece of paper to its matching jagged edge. Sitting cross-legged on the covers, he twisted his pendant mindlessly while he thought about the cryptic poem.

To his surprise the cylinder suddenly fell off his necklace. It must have come off from being twisted so much. He felt the leather cord; the skull was still attached.

What the . . . ? Looking down at his face distorted in the pendant's reflection he realized that the pendant was really a hollow tube. He held it up to his eye. Something was inside.

"No way. Cool!" He turned the tube over and tapped the bottom. A tightly rolled old piece of paper and some dried up round things fell onto his blanket. He rolled one of the dried balls between two fingers, looking at it intently. It was whitish with a dark spot on one side. Big B sniffed it. Fishy. He suddenly realized what it was.

"Gross! Dried fish eyes!" He quickly gathered up the smelly balls and threw them out the window. *What were they doing in my pendant?* he wondered as he wiped his hands furiously on his pants.

He then unrolled the small piece of parchment. The spidery script matched the writing in the ship's log, perfectly. *So this really is Ratbeard's pendant. Cool.*

But what was written on the paper was less obvious:

WILLIAM SHAKESPEARE

HENRY VI

III: I, IV, 35

YORK

"William Shakespeare? What did Ratbeard know about Shakespeare?" Big B thought aloud. He realized he had to go back to the study. His grandpa had to have a book of Shakespeare's works. He'd forgotten to look up the Bible verse, too.

Looking up and down the hallway to make sure the coast was clear he hurried from his room back to the study, and darted inside. After finding a small lamp in the dark, he quickly scanned the titles for the two books he needed. "Aha!" He spied the Bible in the H section for Holy. Reaching up to the highest shelf, he pulled it out and set it upon the giant desk. He closed his eyes for a moment, remembering the verse. *Exodus 7: 19–21.*

He flipped quickly through the pages, finding Exodus close to the beginning. He found chapter 7, and then verse 19: "And all the waters that were in the river were turned to blood. And the fish that was in the river died and the Egyptians could not drink of the water of the river and there was blood through all the land of Egypt."

"Okay, what does that mean?" *It must have something to do with water. Everything lately seems to have something to do with water.* He copied down the verse on a scrap piece of paper.

Big B put back the Bible and moved to the wall that held books whose subjects started with the letter *S*. He read the spines as he scanned the shelves . . . *Salmon's Struggles* . . . *Scavengers of the Deep* . . . *Schematism in Nature* . . . *Scholars of the Renaissance.* His eyes finally spied what he was looking for. Two shelves from the bottom was a thick leather tome, the golden name *The Complete Works of William Shakespeare* stamped onto its spine. *Good thing Grandpa's got such an awesome library,* Big B thought, pulling out the heavy book. He plopped it on the desk and turned the thin pages to the table of contents. He spread out the rolled parchment, tucking each end under the books that were already on the Professor's desk. As he looked at Ratbeard's inky cursive writing his eyes roamed, distracted by the image of a large ship on the cover of one of the books holding the scroll flat on the desk. *The Encyclopedia of Pacific Nautical History* was suddenly more captivating than reading Shakespeare. Curious, he opened the cover and flipped through the text. Boats, compasses, and nautical maps filled the pages. He went further into the book, entertained by its illustrations. A section in the middle of the book displayed glossy full-color pictures showcasing pictures of famous sailors. When he turned to one large portrait his mouth went dry. It was a painting of a man wearing a big ruffled collar, a puffy-sleeved jacket, and calf-length pants. A cape hung from his shoulders. The man's hair was a dark blonde and receding, exactly like Big B's dad's hair, with a matching wispy goatee. Around his neck was an exact likeness of Big B's pendant and on his shoulder perched a dark-grey seagull.

"Ratbeard!" whispered Big B. He read the caption beneath the illustration: "Ratbeard, a.k.a. Sir William Sneath, the most feared pirate of the Pacific from 1581 to 1598, shown with his beloved pet seagull, Krill."

"Krill! It's Ratbeard's seagull! No way!" With renewed interest, Big B looked back at the parchment he'd found inside the pendant.

"Henry VI. III:I:IV:35. Yikes. What kind of code is that?" He looked through the contents of the Shakespeare book and lo and behold, there was *The Third Part of Henry VI*. "Okay, let's find this next message." Big B struggled for a bit, but finally found a verse spoken by the Duke of York. Act I, scene iv, lines 35–39:

```
My ashes, as the phoenix, may bring forth
A bird that will revenge upon you all;
And in that hope I throw mine eyes to heaven,
Scorning whate'er you can afflict me with.
Why come you not? What! multitudes, and fear?
```

Big B was still confused. The words were hard to understand. Not to mention that he wasn't very good in English or spelling, thanks to his habit of always shortcut texting on his cell phone. *Hmmm, texting was sort of like a code*, he realized. He smiled and copied the Shakespearean passage below the Bible verse.

He needed to learn the meaning of the word *phoenix* to help understand the poem. Turning back to the walls of books, he searched again. At last, he spied a thick reddish book with the word *Dictionary* down its spine. He pulled it out and flipped to the *P* section. His finger scanned the pages, hunting for P-h: *phlox . . . phobia . . . phoenix*!

> *phoe nix*, noun: A legendary bird which according to one account, lived 500 years, burned itself to ashes on a pyre, and rose alive from the ashes to live another period.

"A bird that rises alive from its ashes? What's a pyre?" Big B flipped farther into the *P*s looking for the word *pyre*. Along the way his eyes fell upon another word: *prophecy*.

> *proph e cy*, noun: A prediction of something to come

A prophecy. *That's what that story in Shakespeare was! It's Ratbeard's prophecy of Krill. He foretold what was going to happen in the future . . . and the future is now! That bird, his evil seagull, Krill, has come back to life! It has risen from the dead like a phoenix.*

Big B forgot about the word *pyre*, replaced the dictionary, turned off the light, and left the study. He pulled the door shut behind him. Lacking a securing click, it creaked open again. He stared at the door. *Maybe if I can make the door look closed and locked, no one will notice.* He searched for something to put underneath it to keep it from opening. He found a washcloth in the bathroom, wadded it up, and wedged it tightly between door and frame. To his relief, the door stayed in place.

Back in his room, he studied the ship's log again. *So what exactly brought Krill back to life?* He stared at the poem and then the Bible verse.

And all the waters that were in the river were turned to blood.

The verse reminded him of the weird text message he kept getting on his phone and how it unscrambled to become "find the water." He flashed back to being at the waterfall and Sam showing him the farm, and the valley below. He heard her words in his head, "Water is the life-blood of the farm." *Life, blood, water.* He remembered looking through his grandpa's journal, *Advances in Water Webs,* and all the arrows connecting things to each other. *Somehow, all this is related.*

There was that local name Grandpa had circled several times in red: *Ma'ema'e Reef Watershed.* Maybe it, too, was a clue.

Big B studied the paper again with the decoded message.

One by land, three by sea.

By land. By sea. What is by land and by sea? The beach! Big B grabbed his backpack and stuffed the ship's log into it along with the verses and the clue to the Professor's curse. He had to find out where Ratbeard's bones were. He glanced out the window and stopped. It was late and dark. *I should probably wait until the morning,* he thought. He imagined trying to get down to the beach in the dark on the twisty narrow path, and shuddered.

"Tomorrow then," he said, and then crawled into bed, thinking of becoming the hero who would save his grandfather *and* find the pirate treasure.

Chapter 20
Detective Maopopo

W hen Big B awoke in the morning, his first thought was of Ratbeard's bones. He leaped out of bed, threw on some clothes, grabbed his pack and cell phone, and hurried out into the hall. His stomach growled as he opened the garden door. Big B stopped and doubled back to the kitchen, checking on the way to make sure the door to the study was still closed.

Nobody else was around, so he supposed it was all right to help himself to breakfast. In the kitchen, he grabbed two bananas and a hunk of bread, which he wrapped in newspaper, and stuffed them into his backpack. Looking through the refrigerator, he saw the leftover chicken and grabbed a drumstick. As he walked outside, he scanned the sky. No trace of that nasty seagull.

"Who's the chicken now, Krill?" He shook the drumstick at the sky, and then tore off a hunk of meat with his teeth. Big B wiped his greasy mouth on his shirtsleeve and jogged down the path. He picked up the pace, looking down to avoid any tree roots. Suddenly, Sam was in front of him. She looked up, startled as well.

"Sam! I've got to tell you something! I've found something!"

"Yeah, I'm sure you have, you thieving bird!" She glared at him and then sprinted past him toward the house.

"But wait! Sam!"

"Don't *talk* to me!" she screamed and ran faster.

Big B turned back to the path, his shoulders sagging. With a heavy sigh he trotted toward the beach. Before long, he reached the point overlooking Palekaiko Cove, where he stopped to catch his breath. He devoured a banana while staring out at the horizon. Sam's hurtful words echoed in his mind. *You thieving bird!* He squinted like he'd just been slapped.

As he stared out at the ocean, he thought about the stolen necklace. *I was standing right here, looking for the* Bloodlust *. . . and . . . a dark seagull was flying above the cliffs!*

"Krill! That freaky phoenix stole Sam's amulet! That's it!" he shouted.

"That's what?" asked a familiar voice. Nalu was coming up the path.

"Oh, hey, Nalu. I think I know who stole Sam's amulet."

"Good, because she's *huhu*!"

"Hoo-Hoo?"

"Yeah, *really* mad!"

"Uh, yeah, I know."

"Got another banana? I'm starving! Sam made me search every inch of the cove yesterday afternoon and this morning."

"Well, you won't find it down there." Big B handed Nalu his second banana.

"Mahalo, Big B!" Nalu eyed him with interest as he peeled the fruit. "So, who took it?" he asked through a mouthful of banana.

"It's more like *what* took it."

"Dude, why are you being so cryptic? Just tell me."

"Ha! Um, sorry. That's actually really funny . . . cryptic." Big B chuckled, thinking of the codes. "The seagull took it."

"A seagull?"

"Yeah. Ratbeard's seagull, Krill. It took Sam's amulet."

Nalu choked on his banana. He grinned and then burst out laughing. "That is funny, Haole."

"Come on, I'm serious! Where is Ma'ema'e Reef?"

Nalu stopped laughing. "What do you know about Ma'ema'e Reef?"

"I think it's where the seagull must have taken the amulet."

"I have been hearing my dad talk a lot about the reef lately. Dead fish have been washing up on the beach nearby and an unusual kind of fog has been hovering over it. He says that lots of the older locals think the gods of the reef are angry, that they are sending a message. But he doesn't believe that stuff. He thinks something else is going on."

"Nalu, it's not the gods, it's the Bone Pirates! They are here! They've cursed my grandpa and they're coming back for their treasure! And Krill has taken Sam's necklace, the Stone of Souls. They are gaining more strength. We've got to get it back!"

Nalu's eyes grew round. "Whoa! That's heavy! You'd better talk to Sam about *that*."

"She won't talk to me." Big B picked up a pebble and threw it off the cliff. It hit something far below, making a faint noise.

"Write her a note and I'll give it to her. I'll try to explain what you're worried about. She'll listen to me," Nalu offered. "We go way back."

"Good idea." Big B reached into his backpack and tore off a piece of newspaper and wrote:

Sam,

Will you please trust me? I promise, I'll help you get the Stone of Souls back. Please!!!!!

–B

He folded it into a small triangle and handed it to Nalu.

"Tell her we need to hike to Ma'ema'e right away. It's the only way to get back her amulet . . . and my grandpa's mind."

"If you say so, Haole." Nalu took the note. He and Big B walked up the path to find Sam.

"If we find Sam, I'll take off and let you talk to her," Big B said, beginning to see the value of diplomacy.

As they approached the house, they saw Sam. She was standing with Rosa, Armando, Big B's mom, and a very, very big man. They all turned to stare at Big B. Sam's arms were crossed over her chest, and she glared at him.

"Brett, come here, now!" His mom looked mad—possibly madder than he had ever seen her. But she calmed her voice and collected herself. "Let me introduce you to Detective Maopopo."

"Hi, Dad," said Nalu. He glanced over at Big B, who looked back at him, surprised.

Nalu's dad was broad, tall, and muscular with a buzz-cut. He looked tough, ready for pro football. He had odd tattoos winding over the muscles bulging from his arms and showing on his neck above his collar. They reminded Big B of the designs on Nalu's guitar. His eyes were hidden behind mirrored sunglasses.

"The study has been broken into, Brett. There has been some damage," Big B's mom said, very concerned.

Big B hesitated a moment, weighing his options. On the one hand . . . *Oh, well. I'd better tell the truth.* "I know," confessed Big B. "The door. I accidentally broke the lock. I'm sorry."

"The lock is just the beginning, Brett. It's a disaster! There is glass everywhere! Dad's locked cabinet is smashed and his journals are missing! And now Sam says you took her amulet, too? Did you take them? What is going on?"

Big B looked at his mom, shocked. His mouth hung open. Nothing came out. He didn't know what to say. The broken lock must have left the room vulnerable to anyone who wanted to steal the journals. Big B gulped.

"We looked through your room for the missing journals. We didn't find them, but we did find the broken scissors in your desk—the same scissors used to break the lock on the door. Tell us what happened, son."

Big B stared up at Detective Maopopo, frozen. He saw his frightened reflection in the detective's sunglasses, and he imagined the detective's eyes boring into him. He glanced at Nalu and then quickly at Sam.

"Hold on!" he said and ran to his room. Detective Maopopo, and his mom followed. Big B pulled the hidden key out from under his pillow. He held it up.

"Why would I break the glass if I have the key?" challenged Big B.

"Good question. Where did you get that?" responded the detective, studying its shape.

"Um, I don't know, exactly."

"What do you mean, you don't know?"

"Well, it was just in the pocket of my swim trunks. I don't know how it got there."

"Uh-huh. Quite mysterious." said Detective Maopopo, raising an eyebrow. He put his hands on his hips, flexing his enormous muscles in the gesture.

"Do you know where the missing journals are?"

"No."

"Do you know where Sam's necklace is?"

"Well, umm. No."

"Well, I guess for now, we have a mystery on our hands, don't we? If you can think of anything else to tell me, you let me know, eh, Brett?" Detective Maopopo kept the key and turned to leave.

"Make sure you keep an eye on him," he whispered to Big B's mom on his way out.

"Oh, don't worry, Detective. I'm on it!" His mother's expression was not encouraging.

Great, he thought. *How am I going to find Grandpa's mind? Or Sam's amulet if Mom's watching me like a hawk?*

Detective Maopopo popped his head back in the door. "Where did Nalu go? He came in with you."

Big B shook his head and shrugged his shoulders. It was all too much.

"I think I saw him talking to Sam," said his mom, maintaining her watchful eye.

"Thanks." The detective left again.

His mom took a deep breath. "You're . . ."

"I know," said Big B, "I'm grounded. What else is new?"

"That's quite enough, Brett. You have behaved very badly."

"There's more to it—if you'd let me explain . . ."

"Not now, Brett. I want you to stay in your room and think about what's happened."

"Don't worry. I will." He could feel his mother's eyes on the back of his head as he crept to his room. He fell backward onto his bed and covered his face. He could hear his mom pull his bedroom door closed and walk up the hall.

Big B stared at the ceiling, trying to figure out what to do next, how to convince Sam, how to get out of his prison sentence so that he could find the pirates. Unfortunately, all that thinking didn't help much. *Dark's bright star* wouldn't lead him anywhere from his room as long as he was grounded.

The morning passed slowly. Big B spent more time examining the ship's log, but he couldn't find any more clues to help him decipher the verses or the passage. Sometime after noon, there was a knock at his door.

"Yeah?" he called out.

To his surprise, Sam opened the door. She stood in the hallway, holding a tray with food. "I brought you some lunch," she said without looking at him.

"Oh. Thanks." Sam didn't respond right away. The silence stretched on. Finally, she looked up and met his gaze.

"I'm sorry, Big B. Really sorry. Sorry I didn't believe you. Sorry I told Detective Maopopo I thought you stole my necklace."

"That's okay."

"No, it's not. I shouldn't have jumped to conclusions. Nalu told me what you told him. I should have listened to you."

"Well, how about now?" Big B asked. "Do you want to see what I found?"

"Yeah!"

Sam set the tray down and sat on the desk chair. Big B opened the ship's log and showed Sam the verses and the torn piece of paper he'd found in his grandfather's study with the poem about the curse and the antidote. He also showed her the quotes from the Bible and Shakespeare's *Henry VI,* and told her about the portrait of Ratbeard with Krill.

"I can't believe that crazy seagull is Krill," Sam said, eyes wide and head shaking. "I just can't believe it."

Big B then showed her the picture he'd taken on his cell phone of the strange image he'd found in the book.

"Do you know what that is?"

"Hmmm . . . no," said Sam, squinting as she looked at the image.

"I think if we can get to Ma'ema'e beach tonight, when we can see the stars, we can figure it out."

Big B's mom appeared in the doorway. "Oh, hi, Sam." She didn't seem very pleased to find Sam and Big B talking in his room.

"Uh, hi, Mrs. Harrington."

"It was kind of Sam to bring you lunch," she said, giving Big B a suspicious glance.

"*De nada,*" Sam said. "And I don't think Big B took my amulet after all."

"Really? Well, that's good news, I think."

"See, Mom, I told you!"

"Okay, honey, you didn't take the necklace, but that doesn't let you off the hook for your grandpa's study or the journals."

"Mrs. Harrington, I think we can prove that Big B didn't take the journals and I think we can find my necklace, but I'll need his help."

"I'm sure that would be very nice, dear," Big B's mom replied, distractedly. "I'll think about it tomorrow. Tonight I'm taking Dad to his awards ceremony in town and I expect Brett to stay in his room."

"Mom—!"

"No. In your room. You're grounded, remember?" She added, "And don't entertain him too long, Sam." With that Mrs. Harrington left the room.

They sat silent until her footsteps faded away.

"Now what?

By an exchange of glances and shrugs, Big B and Sam agreed on what they had to do. And they were sure Nalu would help.

Chapter 21
Falling Ashes

B ig B felt bad about planning to betray his mother's trust. However, it did seem as though Nalu's island gods had arranged for Grandpa to be honored at a big awards dinner this particular night. Armando would drive them and Rosa was going along to visit her sister in town.

For the rest of the afternoon Big B rechecked his gear for the hike out to Ma'ema'e Reef. He emptied and then repacked his backpack for the third time, worried that he was forgetting something. First, he repacked the ship's log. He tucked the torn piece of paper with the message protectively between the log's pages. Wrapping the tattered old book in a towel, he slid it into the pack. Next he checked that the picture he'd taken was still saved to his phone. He unfolded the T-shirt he had wrapped around the magnifying glass to protect it, cleaned the glass with a corner of the shirt and then bundled it up again. He slipped both the phone and his magnifying glass inside the front pouch of his backpack. He then changed into jeans, a red hooded sweatshirt, and his wrestling shoes.

Next, Big B delicately picked up the empty vial that had held Armando's cleanser and took it into the bathroom and rinsed it out. He filled the glass tube with water and held it up to the light. No face emerged. Big B poured out the water, capped the top, and dried off the outside. He carried the vial back to his room, unzipped the backpack's front pouch, and slid it inside. Finally, he tucked the paper with the verses he had copied into the front pocket of his jeans.

At five o'clock Big B's mom poked her head into his doorway to say good-bye. She looked very fancy but not very happy. "You will stay in this room and out of trouble, Brett. If I could stay—" but at the sound of a beep from the driveway she just ended with "Be good, see you later." He heard the engine start and the wheels crunch. He was free. *Touchdown!* He threw his pack over one shoulder and hustled to meet Sam outside.

———

She was already sitting on the porch steps, waiting for him. "Ready to go, Gallo?"

"As ready as you are, Grape Ape."

"Let's go then."

"Where's Nalu?"

"You'd better call him."

"But my cell phone doesn't have any coverage."

"Call him the Nui way." Sam looked over at the conch shell sitting on the porch, and Big B's eyes followed.

"No way."

"Come on, Pollo, we have to hurry!" Big B picked up the shell and held it to his lips. He tried with no luck. He tried three times, but on the fourth attempt a deep resonating uuuuuuuuueeeeeeeee! Echoed down the valley.

"Now that was da bomb!" Sam smiled big. The breeze picked up, catching her hair. Her long purple locks floated up in the wind. Big B went pale, remembering his dream of Sam as the figurehead, her watery hair floating in midair.

"What's the matter?" asked Sam, seeing Big B's face change color.

"Um, nothing." But the hairs on his arms were standing on end.

"Looks like you've got chicken skin, Pollo!" Sam laughed and pinched his arm. "Like you've just been plucked!"

"Ow!" Big B rubbed the red spot on his arm.

Sam and Big B started walking briskly down the beach path. Big B's skull-faced pendant bounced to the rhythm of their steps.

The palm trees swayed and the bushes danced in the wind. The sky glowed pink and the clouds were brilliant orange, painted by the setting sun. It reminded Big B of a swirling scoop of rainbow sherbet. There was a feeling of energy in the air. Or maybe it was just the nervous expectation of this night's promise. Finding the Bone Pirates—and hopefully finding the Stone of Souls, his grandpa's mind, and some buried treasure, too! Suddenly he remembered the Professor's missing journals.

"Hey, Sam?"

"Yeah?"

"You told my mom we could prove I didn't take Grandpa's journals. Do you really think we can?"

"Sounded good at the time, didn't it? But I don't know. A lot of people would like to get their hands on those journals. People who are very much alive."

Big B was suddenly startled by an unexpected flying object. "Hey, I thought the bats came out after dark!"

"They do." Sam seemed puzzled. They looked up into the rosy sky. A shrill cry pierced their ears. Big B knew that sound. A dark grey bird dive-bombed him. It pecked at his chest, as before, in an attempt to snatch the pendant. Then it aimed for his face, its beak snapping at his eyes. Punching back furiously, Big B managed to fight the bird off.

Krill rose in the air and circled overhead, staring at them through his blue glowing eyes. It dove again, pecking, and getting its feet tangled in Sam's hair. She screamed, waving her arms wildly, batting at the creature. She smacked the attacking gull with a fierce jab from her elbow, sending it reeling into the air. With a beak full of purple hair, it flew off into the sunset.

"Are you okay?" asked Big B, stunned.

"I'm going to kill that flying rat!" Sam shook her fist at the sky. Her eyes filled with tears and she looked away. She wiped her eyes on her sleeve, rubbed her scalp, and took a deep breath.

"I'm okay, though." Sam took another breath, closed her eyes, and collected herself. Big B watched her worriedly. Her hair was a nest of tangles from the scuffle. He noticed a dark feather caught inside the twisted purple strands.

"Hey, there's a feather in your hair!"

She opened her eyes. "Get it out! It's probably diseased."

Big B reached into her hair and pulled it out. He held it up between them. The dark feather was unusual. It was opalescent, reflecting rainbows, like an oil spill. When the sunlight hit it, it glowed orange and red, shimmering like a flame. A gust of wind blew, and the feather tilted in Big B's fingers. For a moment, it looked like fire blowing in the wind. He could see Sam's intrigued expression through its gauzy form. The wind blew again, but from a different direction. Grey clouds passed overhead. Suddenly, a sharp hot pain zapped Big B's fingers. A gust of wind tore the feather from his fingers and sent it spiraling away from its captors.

Big B ran after the feather, grabbing and jumping at it. He looked like a cat chasing a toy. Sam ran after him, cheering him on.

"Get it! You almost had it! Hurry!"

In one last attempt, Big B threw his body into the wind and stretched his arm as far as it would reach. Miraculously, he snagged the enchanted feather before it could escape, and he fell to the ground, landing on a big spiky plant.

"Ouch!" He scraped his hand against its jagged edges as he struggled to get free. Before examining his wound, he stuffed the prized feather into his backpack and zipped the pocket securely shut. Big B's fingers were black with ash. He sniffed the fine soot as he rubbed them together. It smelled burned.

"Gotcha!"

"Boy, you certainly know how to pick the right plant to land on," Sam laughed.

"You mean the vicious ones with big teeth?"

"Well, at least *this* plant can apologize for wounding you." Sam broke off the tip of one of the plant's leaves. She squeezed out its clear sap and rubbed it on Big B's sooty scratched hand. "You've probably heard of this plant. It's aloe vera. The locals here call it *panini 'awa'awa*, or cactus medicine."

"Cool. Maybe you are a healer after all, even without the Stone of Souls."

Just then a shrill cry echoed from off in the trees.

"Krill." They said in unison.

Chapter 22
One by Land, three by Sea

they took off down the trail. Nalu was waiting for them at the surfboard shed.

"Hey, it's about time! If we don't hurry we'll run out of light." Nalu put his hands on his hips. He looked like a younger version of his dad, Detective Maopopo.

"Don't overdo it, Nalu!" Sam said, laughing. "It's okay, I brought a flashlight." She pulled a flashlight out from the pocket of her cargo pants.

Nalu led the way up the beach. He was wearing island print pants. Big B noticed a wad of green leaves sticking out the back pocket of his pants.

"What is that? Island toilet paper?" Big B teased.

"What?"

"Those leaves, in your pocket, Nalu. Are they for your little animal buddies?"

"Oh, those. They're ti leaves. They come from the ki plant."

Sam put her hand over her mouth and laughed.

"What?" asked Big B unaware of the joke.

"I thought you didn't believe in the Bone Pirates, Wanana." Sam poked at him. "Ti leaves are used to ward off evil spirits," she explained to Big B. "I guess Nalu, here, is beginning to believe us."

"I figured it couldn't hurt," Nalu shrugged and smiled. He turned back around to walk faster. "My folks keep talking about Ma'ema'e Reef. My tutu is convinced the gods are angry again. She believes the Bone Pirates have been disturbed."

Big B looked at Nalu.

"She's right. They've got to be there, near the reef. How far is it?"

"Ma'ema'e is two coves after this one. It's on the other side of that rocky point." Nalu pointed toward the end of the island. "But it's not as close as it looks."

"Come on, we better get moving." A deep red had begun to creep onto the horizon. It trailed behind the sun as the earth spun them away from the light of day. The three walked quickly to the outcropping that separated Palekaiko Cove from the next cove and scrambled over the rocky point. As soon as they reached the sand on the other side, they jogged along the beach toward the next rocky outcropping that blocked the view of Ma'ema'e Cove.

Big B was surprised by how hard it was to run in the sand. He couldn't go very fast, and his muscles were burning before they were halfway across the beach. When they finally got to the rocks, Nalu led them up the rough volcanic surface of the rocky point. It was very steep and at least two stories high. Waves crashed against the half-submerged boulders below, launching an occasional misty spray over their heads. Big B, thankful for the grip of his wrestling shoes, climbed carefully over the highest point to reach Sam and Nalu. He looked ahead and saw it: the white sandy crescent of Ma'ema'e Cove sheltered by a sheer cliff that must have been a hundred feet high, rising up from the point. He stopped to catch his breath and looked up at the stars that had begun to appear.

He took off his backpack and pulled the decoded, cryptic message out from the pages of the towel-wrapped ship's log. It was tough to read in the deepening dusk, so Sam flicked on her flashlight.

"Thanks. See if this means anything to you guys. 'One by land, three by sea. In line with dark's bright star. I will wait for thee.'"

"You got me," Nalu said scratching his head with a ti leaf. "Maybe we need to find one thing on land and line it up with three things in the sea. We just have to find the *things* we're supposed to line up."

Sam looked up. "There's your star." She pointed to the brightest star twinkling in the dusky sky. "Sirius."

"I believe you," said Big B.

"No, silly. That's the name of the star. It's spelled S-I-R-I-U-S."

"Oh. Seriously?" Big B was amused by his pun.

"Now we just have to find the *other* things," said Nalu, frowning in concentration.

As Big B was about to zip the paper back in his pack, he stopped. Way out on the horizon of the ocean, he saw a group of islands. They were barely backlit from the last deep-red rays of the setting sun. The islands looked as though they were floating in fire. He pointed to the ocean.

"Hey, Nalu."

"Yeah, Haole?"

"How many islands are out there?" Big B pointed to the horizon.

"Oh, way out there? You mean the Kahikolu . . . of course, yes, the Kahikolu!"

"I don't know what that means."

"*Kahikolu* means 'trinity,' you know, three!"

"Right, Nalu!" Sam grinned with excitement. "Now we just have to find the *one* other thing."

Nalu and Sam scaled down first and jumped onto the soft sand. Nalu unrolled the ti leaves from his back pocket and tucked one between the rocks behind them.

"What's that for?" asked Big B as he hopped down past them.

"To get back safely."

Sam and Big B looked at each other, apprehensively. "Are you guys ready?" Big B asked, looking at Sam and Nalu.

"Yeah, let's do it," said Nalu, squaring his shoulders.

The three of them headed out across the beach at a steady lope. Approaching the far side of the cove, they stopped, breathing hard from their long run.

"Hey, look at that!" Sam pointed to a dark lump on the beach.

"Ee-yew! Nasty! It's a dead fish," said Big B, catching up.

"The gods *are* mad!" said Nalu, nervously looking around. He covered the fish with one of his ti leaves. "Look, there's more. Hundreds. I don't have enough leaves to cover them all."

Sam shivered as a thick mist blew in over the rocky cliffs from the adjoining coves. The wind whipped her hair. Clouds suddenly began billowing in, darkening the landscape.

Big B pulled his hood up. "We better find our way soon before this storm comes in. I think we've found the *three by sea*. Now let's find the one."

They turned around and scanned the land behind them.

Big B looked at Pukaaniani, the Window. The rock arch rose up from the cliffs at the far point of the beach; a misty fog poured through its opening.

Big B slid his backpack around and fished out his cell phone from the pocket. He flipped it open and the image of the arch came up on the screen.

"Hey!" Big B started jogging toward the rock. "Follow me!"

Charged with sudden realization and anticipation, he outran them both across the rest of the beach. Without stopping, he scrambled up the rocks to the base of the huge volcanic arch. He slowly looked up in awe as he stepped under it, barely noticing the strange burning in his throat each time he breathed in. Sam and Nalu caught up to him.

"I would say this looks like a 'one,'" said Sam, looking up.

"Actually, it's like we're standing right in the 'O!'" said Nalu.

The three of them stood side by side, looking out through a break in the mist. They watched the three islands slowly disappearing into the dark blue arrival of night.

Big B looked up at Sirius showing dimly in the cloudy sky, and then out at the islands, confirming his hunch. "The islands, the arch, and the star line up as if an imaginary line was drawn through them." Sam and Nalu followed Big B's finger, turning around to face Nui Island as he drew an imaginary line in the night sky, connecting the two landmarks with the star.

He held up his cell phone showing his friends the image compared to the view through the arch. The conical black silhouette of Makemake rising in front of them, Magma's youngest volcanic daughter, matched the image perfectly.

"Think big," whispered Big B.

Chapter 23
the Land of the Bone Pirates

S am and Nalu stood next to Big B as he held up the phone under
the towering rock arch. A wave crashed behind them, sending
salty spray spattering around them, while they studied the image
on the tiny screen.

"Hey," said Nalu, "I bet those four squiggly lines are the hot
springs."

"Hot springs?"

"Yeah, there are four pools of water on this side of Makemake, about
a mile or so up. They are heated from below by the power of the volcano. The first spring is right up there," Nalu said as he pointed up the

hill from the arch. "We just follow the creek up. I haven't been there since last summer. It's really palekaiko up there."

They scrambled up the hill, hopping back and forth across the creek. The higher they climbed, the more Big B's eyes and throat burned and itched. He cleared his throat frequently, and he heard Sam and Nalu doing the same. He focused on his footing, fighting off the fear rising inside him; he had no idea what lay in store for the three of them. It occurred to him, briefly, that his mother thought he was safe in his room.

Everything had grown eerily quiet and dark. Sam lit their path through the misted air, her light reflecting off the floating water particles.

As they crested the top of the hill, they walked through billows of steam that made it difficult to see. A sudden gust of warm wind cleared the view before them and delivered a foul stench to their noses.

"Here's the first hot spring," said Nalu, pointing just up the hill. "Funny, it smells different from what I remember." The spring gurgled and bubbled like soup simmering on the stove.

"There's another one just up there, and then two more a little beyond that." Nalu pointed up the path to a higher plateau. They quickly hiked up to the next level. Steam rose from another bubbling pool of water. Sam shone her flashlight around. The landscape was stark and rocky.

"Something's definitely different," Nalu said, looking around. "I used to swim right here. It's been a while, but I remember it being much greener, you know, more plants and stuff. And it had lots of flowers, too. And frogs. And now I don't hear any frogs . . . or crickets."

Nalu blew his whistle. Nothing responded. "I wonder what's going on."

He walked briskly up the hill, a concerned look on his face. Sam shone her light ahead, guiding his way. Nalu stopped. Two blue orbs glowed back at them. Krill. The seagull hopped toward them and screeched.

"Looks like *something* answered my call!" hollered Nalu over his shoulder.

Big B leaped at Krill and yelled, waving his arms. The bird recoiled and flew away to safety. It leered at them from a rock farther up the path.

Sam cast her flashlight beam along the last plateau. Her light revealed more and more eyes. There must have been a hundred sets of eyes— the dark, black, empty eyes of skulls staring back at them and reflected in scattered pools of stagnant water.

To make the setting even more creepy, eerie sounds murmured from the steaming vents, and they noticed that someone had laid out bones on the ground as if trying to form a complete skeleton. Their hearts raced faster.

Nalu stared in horror. "I never knew these bones were here. And why are there so many clamshells this high up?" He kicked at one of the clamshells and Sam followed it with the beam of her light, revealing hundreds more spread out over the plateau.

Nalu continued. "This plateau used to be entirely covered with plants and trees and living things. It was so beautiful. With the plants gone, the soil must have eroded off the side of the mountain. These skeletons must have been buried here for hundreds of years."

"It *is* the Bone Pirates," whispered Sam.

Big B pulled the message back out of his pack and spread it out so that Nalu and Sam could read it in the flashlight's beam.

ONE BY LAND, THREE BY SEA
IN LINE WITH DARK'S BRIGHT STAR
I WILL WAIT FOR THEE
ONE WILL BE, MANY YOU'LL SEE
BUT THE KEY TO MY RICHES

Lies beneath me

Seek wisely or dread
You will lose your head
And your thoughts within will flee
For time you will dwell
Sealed like pearl in your shell
While our spirits in our bones go free

If attacked by my curse
You may feel even worse
To know I have left you the cure
But this antidote creeps
While your mind begs and weeps
From the poison that plagues your bright shore

They scanned the graveyard. "What are we looking for?" Sam shone her light at the masses of empty faces.

"Ratbeard" Big B said. "It lies beneath him."

"Which one is Ratbeard?" Sam held her flashlight tightly as she scanned the bones. *Splash, splash, splash,* tumbled the water. *Hisssss,* whispered the springs.

Krill screamed at them from a large rock, "Ki-yah!"

"There." She said illuminating the gull. "I'll bet Krill is guarding him."

"Brilliant. That's it! I'll bet you're right, Sam. Come on!" The bird began to hiss as they came closer.

Suddenly Sam stumbled and fell, and Big B and Nalu heard the sounds of the metal flashlight striking a hard surface, the crunch of breaking bones, and a shrill screech as Krill darted away. They cringed.

"You okay, Poni?"

"Yeah, I'm fine. But ee-yew! This stuff stinks. It's all over me." From the ground, the flashlight illuminated a small cloud of green dust floating over the cluster of bones and broken clamshells.

Sam sneezed as Nalu helped her up. "It's okay, Sam. Come on. Let's go see what Krill was guarding."

Big B returned the flashlight to Sam, and she used it to scan the area around them to see what she had tripped over. Nalu kicked another skull slightly, crushing a shell beneath it, spewing out a puff of powder. He quickly jumped back and then stood very still.

"Be careful! Don't touch anything. The shells are booby-trapped."

Chapter 24
Ratbeard's Remains

"K i-ya!" Krill shrieked.

Big B scanned the bone yard looking for Krill. He could hear, even feel him swooping around them. Sam's flashlight cut wildly through the air, showing nothing but a dull beam of empty light in the grey mist, and then something caught Big B's eye. A little farther up the hill a sapphire blue glow flashed in the beam of Sam's light.

"Let's keep going up," suggested Big B, "but watch your step." The acrid odor in the air got stronger the higher they climbed.

After several minutes, they stopped in front of a gurgling pool. Tiny luminescent spots of light glittered in the water as it flowed over the pool's rock edges and poured into the creek that it fed.

Sam pointed the flashlight into the dark spring. There seemed to be a hole at the bottom where the water bubbled up from underground.

"This is the source," Nalu whispered, reverentially.

"The life blood." Big B bent over to get a closer look, and out of the corner of his eye he saw a cool blue light shining from behind a pile of large rocks. Krill screamed and landed in front of the rocks, blocking Big B's view. The bird walked back and forth in front of the rock pile, hissing and snapping at them.

Big B leaped at Krill with his arms wide and hollered, "Go back where you came from, nasty zombie bird!"

Shrieking, Krill flew off into the fog.

Big B circled the pile, and then knelt in front of the glowing rock. It wasn't a rock at all. It was a skull.

"Well, well. Captain Ratbeard, I presume? I believe you may have something we're looking for." Big B reached into the eye socket of the skull and pulled out Sam's glowing necklace, the Stone of Souls. Sam was having trouble holding the flashlight steady.

"Once a pirate, always a pirate!" Sam said, feeling both anger and relief.

A deafening rumble thundered through the clouds above. Raindrops began pelting down on them. Sam tried hard to hold the light steady as she trembled. Big B noticed that something else had caught the light from within Ratbeard's mouth.

He reached in between the skull's yellow, decayed teeth, knocking one out with a brush of his hand. He touched something hard and cold. He flinched and pulled his fingers back. The clouds rumbled again and the rain fell harder. Water dripped off the skull like tears.

"But the key to my treasures lies beneath me," Big B said aloud. Still holding Sam's necklace in one hand, with the other he pulled up the skull and set it aside. It rolled and tumbled into the pool where more bones were submerged. A dark rectangle protruded from the mud where the skull had sat. Big B began to dig it out.

Once he had freed the object, he wiped off the greenish mud, revealing a tarnished silver box with a porcelain lid. He stuffed the box into his backpack and leaned over to wash off his hand in the pool. Just as he was about to plunge his hand into the water, its stench made him change his mind. Suddenly, the anagram flickered in his mind. *FIND THE WATER.* Big B stared deep into the pool.

"What are you doing?" Sam shone the flashlight right into Big B's face.

"I don't know . . . yet!" he shouted back over the wind and rain.

Lightning brightened the sky. A crooked finger of electricity arced through the air, momentarily turning the black night into a luminous blue. Thunder boomed as the sky went dark again.

"Come on guys, that was close!" yelled Nalu.

Without hesitation, Big B pulled out the empty vial from his backpack. He leaned back over the pool to fill it with the disgusting liquid spewing from the ground. The water wasn't warm like the hot springs. It was cold, and it smelled like sewage, with a hint of something that smelled sort of like gasoline. Trying one-handed to cap the vial, he dropped the Stone of Souls. It bounced into the pool next to Ratbeard's skull. "Oh no." He capped the vial and tucked it into his pocket. As he knelt down to retrieve the necklace, his body froze.

Everything turned a blinding white. The air sizzled. A bolt of lightning struck the pile of rocks between the spring and the pool, throwing Big B forward, across the toxic water.

Big B lifted his head, feeling a buzz in the air. His hair stood on end, bathed in static. The pool was lit with an electric blue light that traveled along a current through the stream, lighting each one of the hot springs and the rest of the stream all the way down the hillside. Finally it entered the sea far below them. The vivid blue light swirled out into a glowing whirlpool, illuminating Ma'ema'e Reef.

Glowing blue steam hissed from the lit water and twirled up, dancing in the wind. Big B heard a whisper in his ear.

"Whoooossse the pirate nowwww?" The voice cackled a menacing laugh.

Big B looked into the pool and watched, petrified, as the form of a face appeared around Ratbeard's skull, shifting and floating in translucent blues. The head rose up, lifting above the pool of water, forming itself from the drops of heavy pounding rain. The raindrops smashed into Sneath's liquid head, forming craters in his ghostly apparition, then dripped off his pointed glowing beard. Sam and Nalu saw the pirate's body slowly rising next to Big B. Neither could speak. Big B's mind screamed "Run!" but he couldn't move a muscle.

Hanging around the neck of the rising Ratbeard was the Stone of Souls. It flickered dozens of shades of electric blue. In a flash Big B realized that the Stone of Souls turned blue when the pirates were near.

"B-B-B-Beee! R-r-r-run!" Nalu yelled.

Just as Big B was about to turn and run, he reached out and yanked the necklace away from Ratbeard. The chain sliced though the pirate's watery neck. Ratbeard's head wobbled, fell off to the side, and then tumbled off his rising body. But Ratbeard's rising wet hand caught it and placed it back on his own shoulders. He smiled and let out a deep and diabolical laugh.

"Come on! Let's go!" screamed Nalu.

"I can't!" Sam cried.

The steam rising beneath her feet had formed a misty hand, its bony fingers curled around her ankle. The shape of a grotesque pirate emerged underneath the rising hand, his leering face whipped and twisted by gusts of wind. Nalu reached down and pulled with all his strength, freeing her leg.

More pirates began to materialize, some crawling out from puddles and rising as dripping masses of glowing water. Others fluttered and twisted as electrified steam. Big B moved closer to Sam and Nalu. They formed a triangle, and the pirates circled, closing in on them from all sides.

Lightning cracked again. The pirates dripped and hissed, slowly coming closer. Big B took a deep breath and clenched his fists. He had to think fast. With a holler, he charged at one of the pirates, slamming into it as if it had been a linebacker. It exploded into a sizzling cloud of water and steam. The apparition had burned his shoulder, but he'd broken a hole in the closing circle.

"Come on!" he screamed.

As Sam and Nalu raced through after him, a shrill cry came from Krill, circling just above their heads. Nalu grasped his shell whistle and blew as loud as he could. But it didn't work. Krill dove among them again and again. Just as his ice-blue eyes homed in on the necklace in Big B's hand, a thick cloud of flapping black wings enveloped the bird in their dark mass.

"Cave bats!" Big B yelled triumphantly.

"Go!" Nalu yelled.

The three turned and ran as fast as they could, heading down the hill. The pirates floated behind them, traveling through the pouring drops of rain. The heavy rain had started to collect and had begun gushing down the hillside in rivulets. The torrents combined, creating stronger and more violent flows. The pirates followed, moving through the streams down the trail, grabbing for Sam's, Nalu's, and Big B's ankles.

They ran like crazy, hearts pounding, slipping and sliding down the slick, muddy path.

"We've got to find shelter!" Nalu yelled.

Sam suddenly took the lead. Stumbling from the path, she sprinted and leaped over rocks and plants. She then scrambled over a pile of rocks and disappeared.

Big B and Nalu followed until they lost sight of her.

"Here!" They heard Sam's voice from a dark opening within the rock, followed by a sneeze.

They slipped in, one at a time, through the hole. Inside, Sam shone the light around to reveal a cavernous room. It was dry and felt secure from the rain pounding down outside.

Big B peeked outside. "Nice job, Sam. I think we're safe." Just as the words left his mouth, the three of them saw a wet hand forming in the water that trickled into the cave.

"Hoopee! Frock the bopening!" ordered Sam.

Big B and Nalu looked at each other, shocked.

"Curry!" They quickly jumped into action, collecting and gathering rocks from inside the cavern, and piling them into the crevice to form a blockade. Misty hands reached through the cracks. Sam and Big B slapped handfuls of mud between the gaps while Nalu stuffed in the last of his ti leaves. The pirates were sealed outside, away from them. And Big B, Sam, and Nalu were sealed . . . inside.

The only sound in the cave was their own heavy breathing and heart-beats thumping in their ears. Bathed in the light of Sam's flashlight, the cavern glowed a warm yellow. It seemed safe. They finally began to re-lax. "Here you go, Sam. I think this belongs to you," said Big B, holding out the Stone of Souls.

Sam hung it around her neck and sniffled. "Meddling supersize meez."

Big B and Nalu looked at her, speechless.

The flashlight flickered, and then went out.

Chapter 25
Caved In

S am desperately tried to shake some light from the dead flashlight, but it was useless. The three huddled together, shivering in the dark. The rain drummed outside and echoed against the walls of the rocky chamber. The darkness seemed to amplify all of the sounds.

"Oh, for Magma's sake, what are we going to do?" Nalu's voice bounced around the cave. The question sent a chill down their three wet spines.

Suddenly, the Stone of Souls around Sam's neck began to sparkle red. The light intensified, illuminating the cave.

"Sam, are you feeling okay?"

"Yeah. I think so."

"Umm . . . you said something about 'meddling meez.'"

"Did I?"

Suddenly it seemed clear to Big B: "It must have been the powder in the clam shells under the skulls. It must be what happened to Grandpa! The green powder must be the curse. Your Stone—I think it's healing you. And now it's red. Your grandma—must be helping."

"Whose grandma?" Nalu was confused.

"You know, Isabella, Sam's grandmother. She gave Sam the Stone, and it has special powers. It glows blue when weird stuff with Ratbeard is about to happen and red when her grandmother is trying to help us, like now."

"He's right, Nalu, it's true." Sam glowed red like the Kahikolu at sunset. "And I do feel better."

Big B heard a beep from his backpack. He unzipped the pocket and pulled out his cell phone.

"And check this out! Isabella uses my cell phone to send us messages. See?" Big B opened his phone and held it up for Nalu to see. Nalu shrugged.

"I don't see anything."

Big B was confused. There was nothing but a blank white screen.

"Wait. There's always a message. I don't get it." He pushed the buttons desperately, hoping to receive Isabella's help, but the bright screen only illuminated his disappointed face.

"Well, looks like we at least have a working flashlight," Nalu observed cheerfully.

"You're right! See, she is trying to help us!" Big B held up the phone victoriously, lighting the cavern walls, and the ground around them.

"Look. There's a pick, and shovel, and brushes."

Sam stood, "Those are the Professor's. He must have been here." She picked up the tools and zipped them into her pack.

"Look familiar?" Big B picked up a dark feather, exactly like the one he had collected from Krill. Sam nodded.

Big B held the phone up to light the ceiling. Hundreds of bats hung upside down. "Wow."

"Hey, Sam? How did you know how to find this cave?" Nalu asked, impressed and thankful for her quick rescue.

"Well, when I saw the cave bats come so fast, I knew there had to be a cave nearby. I looked for a break in the foliage and there it was."

"Well done, ke kaikamahine poni. The bats think you are *akamai*," said Nalu. Turning to Big B, he explained, "That means 'very clever.' By the way, what happened up there? That was totally freaky!"

"I don't know, Nalu. I can't explain it. I just had this feeling I should get a sample of that stinking, nasty water, and then everything started happening."

He replayed Ratbeard's whisper in his mind. *Who's the pirate now?*

"We still need to find grandpa's journals. If we really have found the cure, maybe he'll be able to tell us who's taken them."

"If we want to help the Professor, we've got to find another way out." Sam's flashlight suddenly turned back on. They looked at each other knowing they had just received another message. "Come on, we'd better go." They collected their things and began searching deeper in the cave for an alternative way out. Sam aimed her newly functioning flashlight ahead, lighting a path before them.

"Hey, it's getting warm back here," remarked Nalu, who pretended to warm his hands by an invisible fire. "Feels good."

"It's coming from over here." Sam pointed to a side cavern, and the three followed her light inside.

The walls of the cavern were warm to the touch, and the air was thick with moisture, almost stifling. Several bats flew in from behind them, circled above their heads, and then flew out through a hole in the top of the cave. Nalu blew his whistle, and more bats came, swirling about the heads of their guests as if to say hello before heading out to feed. Big B looked up at the crescent moon peeking out from behind swift-moving clouds. The rain had stopped.

"There's our way out," Nalu said.

Sam shone the light along the floor, revealing that they were standing on a ledge. Steam rose beyond the lip of the ledge. They crept up to the edge, and all three gasped when they saw a pool of glowing molten lava far below. Big B had never seen real lava before. It wasn't exactly like Jack's lava lamp. The color was bright orange and black and it bubbled and gurgled, more like hot springs. He could feel its rising heat drying his clothes, hair, and skin.

"I think Magma heard me," said Nalu. "I will let her know we respect her power and are thankful for her guidance."

Nalu removed his precious whistle and dropped it into the molten lava below. With one flare up of fire, the shell was gone, swallowed up by the lava pool.

Big B was dumbstruck. "Why'd you do that? You needed that!"

"Nah," said Nalu. "My tutu says to show respect for the gods with a sincere offering. The gods will honor your sacrifice and your gifts will soon be returned, many times over."

Big B still couldn't believe Nalu had just thrown his magical shell into the fiery hot lava. His phone suddenly beeped. The Stone of Souls flickered red and hot orange, matching the lava below. Big B looked at his phone. Isabella had sent another message, but this time it was obvious. It was the drawing of the *Bloodlust* with one flashing word: DANGER. They looked at one another, fear returning to their eyes.

"We've got to go now!" said Big B. He looked up. "It's the bats' escape hatch or nothing. Who goes first?"

Nalu volunteered to lead the way. Sam illuminated the cavern wall with the beam of her flashlight, and Nalu scaled it by bracing his feet and fingers on the ledges and in cracks. In only a few minutes he had pulled himself up through the opening to the ground outside.

Looking back down through the hole, Nalu called out, "Your turn, Sam!"

Sam handed Big B the flashlight and then began climbing. She moved easily with gripping fingers and light feet.

"Way to go, Spider Monkey!" Big B yelled up in encouragement.

Nalu began yelling, "Hey! Go away! Shoo!"

Sam and Big B could hear shrill cries from above.

Sam, nearly to the top of the opening, yelled to Nalu, "Run! It's Krill!"

The seagull cried at the sound of Sam's voice and dove toward the hole. Nalu lunged at the bird, trying to block its path, but missed. Krill landed on a ledge near the top of the hole and immediately began pecking at Sam's fingers. She struggled to hold on, screaming at the demonic bird. Tiny bits of rock fell, knocked loose by Sam's thrashing legs.

"Hold on, Sam! Hey! Leave her alone, you flying rat!" Big B picked up a rock to throw at it but was afraid of hitting Sam.

"Help!" Sam shrieked.

Nalu's hand appeared through the hole from above as he tried to swat the seagull away. It pecked at and then bit his hand, holding tightly as Nalu tried to fling it away.

"Ow!"

His hand disappeared and Big B could hear him yelling above. Big B tried to distract Krill, who had returned to the ledge.

"Ki-yah! Ki-yah! Here birdie, birdie," he called. He reached into his backpack and pulled out the magnifying glass. He aimed the beam of the flashlight through the glass at the bird. A spot of light pierced Krill's blue eyes.

The bird screeched. It flew past Sam, swooping down into the cavern to confront Big B. It landed on a rock and eyed him. Big B kept the bird in his sight and called out to Sam.

"I'll take care of him—you climb out!"

He saw Nalu reach down to pull Sam free. Krill meanwhile was hopping along the cave floor toward Big B, hissing. He could smell the bird's rotten death-breath. Suddenly, Krill attacked him, flying for his face. Big B covered his face to protect his eyes, but Krill plucked at his skull pendant, attempting to pull it from his neck. Big B swung the flashlight at the creature, sending it reeling toward the opposite wall.

Krill lay dazed on the cave floor for a moment, and then popped up on two feet. Several of its feathers were bent, standing up away from its body. It limped around in a circle several times, and then spread its wings and hissed at Big B. Krill snapped its beak and waddled toward Big B, preparing for its second attack.

"So you want this?" Big B pulled off his pendant and dangled it before Krill.

"Ki-yah!" answered the bird.

He swung it back and forth and Krill's head followed, mesmerized by its gleam.

"Be careful, Big B!" Nalu warned from above.

When Big B glanced up at Nalu, Krill saw his moment of opportunity and went for the pendant. Big B glimpsed the bird's assault from the corner of his eye. At the last second, without thinking about it, he threw the pendant over the rock ledge. Krill dove after it, plunging toward the lava pool. Big B leaned over the edge and watched. Everything seemed to be happening in slow motion. His cherished pendant fell end over end, landing on the orange and black swirling pool of lava, where it seemed to float for a few seconds, teasing Krill. The bird suddenly slowed its pursuit, overwhelmed by the heat. Unfortunately for Krill, it was a few feet too late.

Big B watched in terror as the creature's feathers started to curl and turn black, leaving a twirling trail of smoke from each wingtip. It screeched as it burst into flames, then followed his pendant into the molten lava.

Chapter 26
the *Bloodlust* Attacks

hanks, Magma!" Big B said, startled to hear his own voice echo back at him.

His heart sank, knowing the magical, code-breaking gift that had guided him had melted back into the earth from which it was once born. He imagined the cool polished metal, the sapphire eyes, the silver skull transforming into something unrecognizable. But thoughts about his loss were suddenly pushed out of his mind by the image of Rat-beard's skull transforming into the pirate's ghostly head.

Good riddance! he thought. He zipped the flashlight into his pack and began climbing. Even in the darkness and with the weight of his backpack, Big B easily scaled the wall—thanks to his wrestling shoes. He popped his head out and pulled his body onto the wet grass above.

"Are you okay?" Sam and Nalu asked in unison as they bent to help Big B stand.

"Yeah, I'm good." He smiled victoriously, and then glanced back into the cave. "And Krill, man, that's one Kentucky Fried Phoenix, extra crispy!" The three of them broke into laughter.

When Big B had caught his breath, he gave Sam her flashlight and they walked out on an outcrop so they could see the valley below. The swirling ocean waves glowed the same eerie blue as had the seagull's eyes, Sam's flickering pendant, and the toxic waste flowing into the creek. They headed back to the poisoned creek that led down to the beach.

"Don't step in the water!" Big B yelled back to his friends.

"I'm not stopping in that water, no way," responded Nalu, not quite hearing Big B correctly.

The water wasn't as luminous as it had been, but it still was unusually bright, and it was now coursing in a strong current.

"Wait a minute. What did you just say?" Big B halted abruptly, causing Sam and Nalu, who had been following close behind, to almost run into him.

"What, the thing about stopping in the water?"

"Yeah. Stopping the water." Big B had an idea.

"Come on." Big B started running back up toward the source of the smelly water.

"No way, Haole. We're not going back up there."

"We have to stop it!"

Nalu and Sam looked at each other and then took after Big B, hopping from stone to stone. They arrived back at the hole in the ground, the lifeblood of the stream. Smelly water bubbled up, joining and feeding the rain-swollen creek.

In the light of the moon Big B studied the scene. He thought of school and how Mr. Gruber, his science teacher, had explained that ancient Egyptians used the laws of physics to build the pyramids, moving stones that weighed a ton. A few men could move mountains of stone. Big B found a thick branch and shoved one end under the large smooth rock next to the pool. He rolled a smaller rock under the wood, to be the fulcrum under the middle of his lever. It looked like a seesaw.

"Help me. Now push!" Big B pushed down on the free end of the wood, and Sam and Nalu joined in. The wood crackled. It started to splinter. A deep rumble vibrated lightly under their feet, the sound of stone crunching stone. The rock started to move. "More!" Big B put all his weight on the wood and . . . crack, they all hit the ground. The rock teetered then rolled into the spring, crushing Ratbeard's skull with a loud crunch. Sam shone the flashlight beam into the spring, revealing that the rock had tumbled into the depths, plugging the dark hole.

"Now we can go home," gasped Big B.

The hike down the valley went much quicker than coming up. Everyone was focused on the safety of home. Big B noticed that the blue light in the stream faded more and more as they headed down to the beach. *Maybe the water was somehow feeding the light?*

Sam was the first to run out on the beach, still enveloped by an eerie mist. She suddenly stopped. She turned around to face Nalu and Big B, a look of terror on her face. Her amulet glowed blue.

"Scallywags scramble fur golden squirms!!" The boys stopped short, and stared at Sam, wondering what had happened to her voice. Big B looked beyond her, and then froze, petrified. Through the mist, he saw an enormous black galleon moored at the point. Ratbeard's flag waved, visible through the fog.

A flash of bright blue light exploded from the side of the ship with a deep thundering boom. A glowing blue ball of water arced through the sky, screaming loudly toward them. They cowered down as the whistling light rushed just past them on their left and exploded in the sand. Wet, sizzling sand blasted out in a huge cloud of blue light and rained down around them. It burned their eyes, and the smell was noxious.

"Run! They're firing at us!" Big B realized he was yelling at himself. Sam and Nalu had already taken off down the beach, which the rising tide had shrunk to a thin strip of sand. Big B sprinted to catch up, his heart pounding with fear, seemingly beating faster than his feet moved. Two more watery explosions blasted craters in the sand just behind them. Big B dug his shoes hard into the sand. He could feel it spraying up his back with every sprinting step. A fourth watery cannonball screamed down, barely missing them.

It wasn't until they had reached the cliffs at the end of the cove that they realized they were trapped. The high tide had covered the lower section of rocks that they had climbed over before, blocking their terrestrial escape home. The dark ship's sails were fully inflated and gaining on them through the mist. Another cannon blasted and a screaming ball arced toward them. In a burst that shook the sand under their feet, it crashed into the rocks above. Jets of glowing water and steam blasted out in all directions and then sizzled as they hit the rising black ocean below.

"What do we do?" coughed Nalu.

Big B paced nervously on the beach, running his hands through his hair in concentration. Something snapped under his feet. Then again. Snap, snap, snap! He looked down and saw hundreds of conical shells. They looked exactly like the ones from Nalu's necklace. He held one up and handed it to Nalu.

"I think these are yours!" Big B exclaimed to Nalu, holding out a shell. Nalu looked down and smiled.

"Mahalo, Magma!" Nalu shouted to the volcano.

"Good things come back to you," Big B whispered under his breath.

Nalu rubbed the shell on an exposed rock. He gave it a try, and then rubbed it again.

"Hurry!" yelled Sam. "They're getting closer!" The ship was so close that they could see shapes of watery pirates standing at the helm, cutlasses raised.

Nalu blew. A high-pitched sound came forth. They waited but nothing happened.

"Is it not working because it's a different shell?" asked Big B, anxiously.

"No, it should work. It's the same *kind* of shell." Nalu blew into the shell again.

Suddenly they heard another high-pitched sound followed by several similar cries. They looked toward the water and saw a pod of dolphins. One dolphin moved toward them chirping repeatedly, its body half out of the water.

"Nai'a," gasped Big B.

"Come on!" yelled Nalu to Sam and Big B. "Nai'a and the other dolphins will carry us home." He trudged out through the waves and grabbed the dorsal fin of one of the dolphins.

Sam tossed her flashlight to Big B and ran in after Nalu. Big B stood frozen, looking at the scary black water.

"Come on! It's the water or the ship!"

Another cannon ball of glowing, steaming water screamed down from the sky. But it did not come crashing down. Instead, it spread out into thousands of droplets that rained down. Nalu helped Sam onto the waiting dolphin's back and then pulled himself up onto the back of another. "Hold on tight, Poni!" Sam trembled, but she was able to hold tightly to the dolphin's fin.

Big B quickly shoved the flashlight into his backpack, lifted the bag over his head, and ran courageously into the waves. Nai'a chattered her encouragement and he grabbed on tightly to her fin. Nai'a chattered

again and the pod took off. The prow of the watery galleon came near-
er, looming massively. As Nai'a dragged Big B off, he looked back at the
wooden mermaid, the figurehead leading the ghost boat. He swore he
saw the carved figure's frozen smile turn to a frown as the ship began
to fade.

The dolphins pulled Nalu, Sam, and Big B through the dark currents
and out around the point. The fog slowly lifted the farther they got
away from Ma'ema'e Reef. Riding high on the dolphin's back, Big B felt
as though he were flying just above the water. The cool rubbery skin
pulsed under him as the immense power of Nai'a's muscles rocketed
him forward. He saw another flash from the ship, now shimmering like
a mirage. The ball of water quickly spread into a mist and drifted away
with the wind.

As the dolphins pulled them past the next point, into Palekaiko Cove,
Big B looked back. The ship was no longer behind them. He saw a dull
blue light fading out back in the fog, almost as if it was sinking into the
ocean. Big B smiled. He knew he had cut off their life-blood by sealing
the spring. They cruised across to the far side of the cove where they
had first set out many hours ago. They surfed through the breakers
holding tightly to the dolphin's powerful torpedo-shaped bodies.

"Maholo, Nai'a," Nalu said standing up inside the breakers and bow-
ing in thanks.

Nai'a nodded her head and smiled. Big B held his backpack up over
his head with one hand to keep it dry and let go of Nai'a with the other.
He slipped off Nai'a, landing on his feet in the shallow water.

"Stay away from Ma'ema'e, Nai'a!" Nalu warned. "Tell the others."
Nai'a nodded, understanding. She dove under the water and disappeared
for a long while. The pod followed, jumping out through the waves.

"Bye! Thank you!" yelled Big B. Sam waved as the dolphins disappeared. Her amulet glowed a happy white.

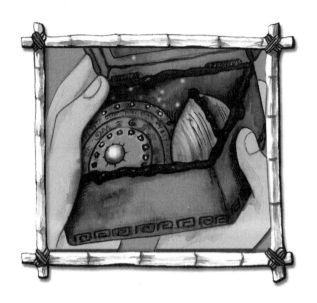

Chapter 27
Breaking the Curse

explaining all this to my father is not going to be easy," Nalu said as he quickened his pace.

Big B put his hand on Nalu's shoulder, stopping him. Big B looked at his two friends, his heartbeat slowing while his mind paused in deep thought. "Wait. Maybe we should keep what we discovered tonight to ourselves. The clue to the treasure is in our hands. And we stopped the water that was polluting the cove."

"Treasure? B, they were firing at us. I don't even want to think about trying to find the treasure." Sam's eyes were wide, fearful.

"Well, I guess we should at least tell someone about the water."

"I agree," nodded Sam.

Their wet clothes stuck to their cold bodies as they jogged, more exhausted then ever, up the beach to the surfboard shed. The closer they got to the small building, the more relieved and safer the familiar place made them feel. A shadow moved suddenly from behind the shed and they froze. Something glinted in the moonlight, and Big B wondered if it could be a cutlass. The shadow came closer until a figure began to emerge in the moonlight.

"Grandpa!" yelled Big B.

"Professor!" said Sam.

"Doc Prune!" grinned Nalu.

The Professor stumbled up to them, moonlight gleaming off his glasses. He was still wearing his baggy old tuxedo with a bright red cummerbund and matching bow tie that had gone askew.

"Wait!" said Big B. He looked at his two friends and they nodded. "We've got so much to tell you!"

He quickly dug through his backpack, handed the flashlight to Sam, and then pulled out the metal box. He showed it to his grandfather.

"Here, Grandpa, sit down." Big B helped his grandfather sit on the soft sand. Sam held the flashlight and Big B read the poem aloud from Ratbeard's journal.

ONE BY LAND, THREE BY SEA
IN LINE WITH DARK'S BRIGHT STAR
I WILL WAIT FOR THEE
ONE WILL BE, MANY YOU'LL SEE
BUT THE KEY TO MY RICHES
LIES BENEATH ME

"That's the clue that connected Pukaaniani with the Kahikolu and Sirius, showing us the way to the plateau. And the clue to the box."

SEEK WISELY OR DREAD
YOU WILL LOSE YOUR HEAD
AND YOUR THOUGHTS WITHIN WILL FLEE
FOR TIME YOU WILL DWELL
SEALED LIKE PEARL IN YOUR SHELL
WHILE OUR SPIRITS IN OUR BONES GO FREE

"That's the clue to finding Ratbeard's skull and the warning of the curse hidden inside the clamshells. Thanks to our fair-feathered friend, we figured that one out."

IF ATTACKED BY MY CURSE
YOU MAY FEEL EVEN WORSE
TO KNOW I HAVE LEFT YOU THE CURE
BUT THIS ANTIDOTE CREEPS
WHILE YOUR MIND BEGS AND WEEPS
FROM THE POISON THAT PLAGUES YOUR BRIGHT SHORE

"The antidote and the key to the treasure must be inside this." Big B held up the metal box. He tried to open the porcelain lid, but it was sealed shut.

"Grandpa. Can I borrow your multi-tool?" Professor Prune gazed at his grandson. He then reached into his pockets and pulled out a toothpick. Then he continued pulling everything from his pockets, dropping the items into a pile on the sand.

"Awesome. Thanks." Big B picked out the multi-tool from the pile and carefully pulled out the blade. The box seemed to be sealed with wax. Big B carved out shards of the wax. When the seal broke, air whispered out. Big B slowly lifted the porcelain lid.

He looked inside, and then at Nalu and Sam. A big smile spread across his face. Sam stared into the box, which was sending off brilliant sparkles of colorful light. Inside was a jewel-encrusted compass. A white pearl crowned its glory. Big B held up the magnificent artifact for all to see.

There was something else. A clamshell sealed in wax, identical to the ones scattered about the plateau. Big B took it out of the box and cradled it in his hands. "I hope this is it. I hope this is the antidote." He carved away the wax then held his face away as he opened the bivalve. Nothing green spewed out.

Big B looked inside. There was nothing but dead ants. "It's gone! The ants must have eaten the antidote!

"No," said Sam thoughtfully, holding her stone, which now glowed red. "That's it! The Professor has to eat the ants. It's literally the *ant-idote!*"

Big B thought she was losing it for sure.

"You better eat some too, Poni," said Nalu, "just in case your Stone of Souls doesn't do the job."

Big B shrugged, "Well, okay. Stranger things have happened tonight than this." He gave Sam a pinch of ants, then held the clam up to Professor Prune. "Here, Grandpa, eat these. They'll make you feel better." Sam ate a small pile of the ants.

"Voot me fly." The Professor took the clamshell and poured all of the remaining dead ants into his mouth. He crunched and then swallowed. A few dead ants remained stuck to his mustache. Grandpa's stomach gurgled. The kids stared at him. The Professor let out a robust burp, blowing his mustache up a little. Big B waited.

"Farton we."

Big B was heartbroken.

"Give it time, Big B, it's got to get into his bloodstream," assured Sam.

Lifeblood thought Big B. He pulled the verses from his pocket.

"Hey, guys, listen to this. Ratbeard left two more clues, one from the Bible and one from Shakespeare."

"Yeah, I remember. You showed me." Sam directed her flashlight toward the scrap of paper and tried to read Big B's handwriting.

"I still don't know what the Bible verse means. Maybe you guys can figure it out." Big B read the verse aloud to Sam and Nalu: "And all the waters that were in the river were turned to blood. And the fish that was in the river died and the Egyptians could not drink of the water of the river and there was blood through all the land of Egypt. —Exodus 7: 19–21."

"No clue, said Nalu.

"I have no idea," said Sam.

"Ingenious!" The Professor suddenly laughed a loud jubilant laugh.

The trio jumped at his unexpected outburst—and then they knew. "Ah, my heroes! I trust you had quite an adventure finding my mind!" The Professor, clear as a bell, was talking normally again, like nothing was ever wrong. The three looked at each other. The antidote must have worked.

Suddenly Big B wanted to share everything. To tell his grandfather all about the strange things that had been happening since he arrived on the island. To explain to his mom why he had to be free for this search. Big B was about to speak, but Nalu put his hand on his shoulder to quiet him.

Nalu laughed, "Well, Doc Prune, evidently we've been trapped in something like one of my tutu's crazy legends."

Sam patted the Professor on the arm. "Nothing a little logic, intuition, and help from some good friends couldn't get us out of."

The Professor slipped the shell into his pocket. "I'll keep this to re-mind me of that little 'pearl of wisdom' or in case I clam up again. He chuckled and then tapped on the box in his grandson's hands. "You kids keep those and see where they take you. Now all you need is a good treasure map."

Sam smiled a huge grin, seeing such a positive change. Nalu's pearly whites glistened in the moonlight and Big B beamed with pride.

"Professor?"

"Yes, Nalu?"

"What exactly did you mean when you shouted, 'Ingenious'?"

"Ah. As I heard my wise grandson here reading the passage from Exodus, everything suddenly all came together in my mind and made perfect sense."

"What did?"

"Ratbeard's curse."

"Read the Exodus verses again, Big B," said his grandpa.

"And all the waters that were in the river were turned to blood. And the fish that was in the river died and the Egyptians could not drink of the water of the river and there was blood through all the land of Egypt."

"I'm convinced that is a reference to a red tide," explained the Profes-sor.

"A red what?" said Big B

"A red tide? That's why all the fish are washing up dead at Ma'ema'e?" asked Nalu.

"Aren't red tides caused by water pollution?" asked Sam.

The Professor wiggled his mustache. "Actually, they are caused by a type of microscopic algae—called a dinoflagellate."

"Dino-flatulence?" asked Big B, confused.

"A dino-flag-ell-ate." The Professor smiled and winked at Big B.

"Some types of dinoflagellates can be very dangerous because they produce toxins that can kill marine life. And some can produce toxins that can affect people."

"Like how?" asked Nalu.

"Burning eyes and throat. Sneezing. A cough. You can feel like you have a bad cold. Severe toxins can affect speech, motor skills, balance, and memory loss, among other things. Very toxic forms can even eat away at the flesh of fish, or even people."

Big B, Nalu, and Sam looked at each other. Everyone looked at the Professor.

"Some are also bioluminescent, meaning they can glow—like a fire-fly.

Like in the spring, realized Big B.

"Add nutrient pollution and they can multiply very rapidly."

"Nutrient pollution?" asked Big B. "Like sewage?"

The Professor nodded. "When conditions are right, dinoflagellates can multiply, or bloom, in enormous numbers. Sometimes their blooms are so large and dense they can be seen by satellite!"

"What does that have to do with Ratbeard's curse?" asked Nalu.

"Well, some toxic dinoflagellates can remain dormant for years in a cyst form that can even survive dried out."

"Like a powder?" asked Sam.

"Yes, Sam. I think Captain Sneath knew something about red tides. We have experienced a particularly dangerous one. A unique one that I have never seen before. He most likely learned of a cure for these toxic dinoflagellates in Panama. Probably from an indigenous tribe as they are usually in tune with nature."

"The ants?"

"I believe so. I do know that tropical leafcutter ants cut little pieces of plants on which they cultivate a garden of fungus in their underground homes. They are like little farmers. Their crop of fungus is sometimes attacked by a mold. But what's really fascinating about leafcutters is that they grow a particular kind of bacteria on their bodies. The bacteria create chemicals that kill the mold that attacks their food."

"Like a medicine, an antibiotic," said Sam.

The Professor nodded. "Maybe the ants we ate tonight were a very special kind of ant, with a very special bacteria on their bodies, or some chemical in them, that somehow counteracted the dinoflagellate poison that was affecting my mind. Maybe. There are millions, no, billions of things nature has to offer us. Nature is complicated. A real mystery. So much to learn."

"Ratbeard was a genius." Big B was amazed by the pirate's knowledge.

"No, Big B. Ratbeard was a pirate who paid attention. Nature is the real genius, my boy. Nature is the genius." The Professor's moustache drew up in a smile.

"Just watch, listen, and learn. And then apply it to your problems," Big B laughed while smiling at Sam.

Sam smirked at Big B. "Oh, Professor. It's so good to have you back!" Sam gave him a big hug.

"One more thing," interrupted Big B. He pulled out the vial of liquid from his backpack and handed it to his grandpa.

"This was coming out of a spring in the hills above Ma'ema'e Reef. It stinks like . . . well, it stinks like sewage and some kind of chemicals. Do you think it's involved?"

The Professor took the tiny vial in his wrinkled hand and looked at it intently through his thick glasses. He slipped it carefully into his pocket. "I'll do some analysis. I have a hunch who might be behind this. Good work, Big B." He patted him on the back.

They knew they had been dismissed when he slowly got up and headed up the path. They heard him saying, "Trust me and do not be deceived, there's plenty more to do."

Chapter 28
Welcome home

They all stood up and tried to brush the sand off their wet clothes. From above in the valley they suddenly heard a deep resonating sound. Uuuuuuueeeeeeeeeee!

"The conch," said Sam, "It's probably my dad. We'd better go!" Sam, Nalu, and Big B followed the Professor up the beach path and headed toward the house.

"Hey, Nalu, stop here for a second." Sam broke off a piece of aloe and squeezed the liquid onto the burn Krill had left on his finger. Big B rubbed a little on his shoulder. They trotted up behind the Professor.

"There they are!" yelled Rosa. "The Professor too!" Armando, Big B's mom, and Detective Maopopo came running outside when they heard Rosa shout.

"Are you kids okay?" asked Rosa.

"We're fine, Mom."

Big B looked at Sam. Her cheery glow had returned to her face.

"Brett Harrington, you have a lot of explaining to do," his mother said. She was still in her long dinner dress but was looking pretty frazzled. "We are going to have a long talk."

"I know, Mom. I'm sorry."

"You weren't the only ones we were worried about. The Professor was missing too! He disappeared after the awards ceremony. Then I noticed the Cruiser was gone too!" Armando emphasized his story with his hands. "We called Detective Maopopo for help, and he found the Professor asleep at the wheel on the far side of the island. Soon after we brought the Professor home, he took off again! We've been worried out of our minds."

Big B swore he heard the faint calling of the cuckoo from the clock from inside the study.

Detective Maopopo spoke up briskly. "We also found two of the Professor's journals in his truck. Here you go, sir. We dusted them for prints and found nothing but yours, I'm afraid. We hope to recover the others for you soon." He handed the journals to Professor Prune.

"Much obliged!" said the Professor, slipping the journals under his arm. "But strangely I think the thief you are looking for may be me."

"Professor! You can talk . . . I mean, you can . . . oh, this is wonderful!" yelled Rosa. She ran over and gave the Professor a hug. "What do you mean, the thief might be you?"

"Well, I vaguely remember, I think, taking the journals."

"To where? asked the Detective.

"I plumb forgot. Of course they're on the island somewhere."

"But why would you break into your own study, sir?"

"I don't know. Yes, why? I must not have had the key. You know things haven't been very clear for me lately. And why didn't anyone tell me I had my pants on backwards?!"

"And you are okay? I mean really okay now?" asked Rosa.

"I feel much better, thank you. My mind is still quite foggy about the past couple of weeks, but my appetite is surely back!"

"You all must be starving. Let's get them something to eat, Rosa," said Big B's mom.

"I'll start the chimenea," proclaimed Armando. Big B's mom and Rosa left for the kitchen while Big B, Sam, and Nalu drifted over toward the little terra cotta stove on the porch. Armando ignited a pyramid of dry twigs, and in no time a cheerful fire bathed the porch in a warm orange glow. Its heat felt surprisingly good in the cool of the late night air. Their wet clothes were drying on their bodies and they were very tired.

Within minutes Rosa appeared with a tray of banana leaves wrapped like packages and put them into the chimenea to cook. Mrs. Harrington brought tall drinks in morning colors.

"What are those wrapped up things?" asked Big B.

"Bananas and chocolate," explained Sam. "We roast them over the fire so they get all warm and gooey. It is *so* good!"

Nalu politely asked through a half-stifled yawn, "So, Mrs. Harrington, how was the awards dinner? Did you have a nice evening?"

Big B's mom glanced sideways at him, looked the three of them up and down as they sat huddled on a bench like refugees from some terrible natural disaster, and said, pleasantly, "Not anywhere near as exciting as yours, I'm sure, Nalu."

You don't even know the half of it, thought Big B, staring into the chimenea.

Rosa returned with a long pair of tongs to remove the roasting bananas from the fire.

"Here, allow me," offered Big B in his most gallant voice.

"Okay, but be careful," warned Sam's mom.

Big B's mom cleared her throat to get his attention. "I *trust* you know what you're doing?" she said with a raised eyebrow.

"Trust me," he said, then carefully fished out the smoldering packages and put them onto Rosa's platter. He got his mother's message. They *would* have a long talk.

After a few minutes, she unwrapped them and passed them around, each with a spoon. One for everyone. Big B took a bite. It was warm. It was gooey.

"Super-choco-banana-licious!" Nalu smiled a chocolatey smile.

"Nui gooey." Big B smiled a similar brown grin.

Big B's grandpa sat next to him. "I've observed that you are no longer wearing your anamorphoscope."

"My what, Grandpa?"

"Your pendant, with the skull. What I had sent to you in a moment of confusion, or maybe inspiration, turned out to be a beneficial decision on my part. I probably would have lost it. Now that my mind is clearing up, I realize it is a code making and breaking device that came to Italy from China in the sixteenth century. Leonardo da Vinci, who was intrigued by the science of optics, had one and drew fascinating cryptic images in his famous notebooks."

Big B lowered his voice though the others were talking among themselves. "I know it can break codes. It helped me find the pirates."

"Did it?" The Professor looked interested.

Big B's voice lowered even more. "Unfortunately I threw it into a volcano."

"Well, that was unfortunate."

"To save a friend."

"Well then, that's fortunate." The Professor patted his grandson on the knee.

"Did you know that the anamorphoscope was hollow?" asked Big B.

"No, I didn't," The Professor's eyebrows tangled together in surprise.

"Yeah, and I found a note, and some dried up old fish eyes."

"Really. I now remember reading a legend that Sneath had trained a seagull, one he named Krill, to pluck out the eye of whoever sought his treasure for themselves. Perhaps they weren't fish eyes after all?" Big B suddenly felt sick. "And what did the note say?"

"It was a clue about something Shakespeare had written. Something about a phoenix rising."

The Professor made a face—the sort of face you made when you remembered something you'd long forgotten. Then he made another, one of understanding. "You have the potential to be a great scientist someday, my boy. Or perhaps even a detective!" The Professor looked up at Detective Maopopo. "Pardon me." His grandfather slowly stood up and walked across the porch.

Or maybe a cryptographer, thought Big B, smiling.

Big B could only partially hear his grandpa, the detective, and Armando talking while looking at the vial. He focused his ears, but only caught a few words: *strange smell . . . chemical analysis . . . investigation . . .* and *grey.*

The detective shook Armando's hand. With a booming voice he called to his son. "Nalu. Time to get home."

"Sam." Armando and Rosa said her name in unison. Sam rolled her eyes. Big B and Nalu laughed.

"See you tomorrow!" Nalu grinned, patting Big B on the back As Nalu was turning away, he stopped and grabbed Big B by the shoulder. "Hey, we need to get you a board!"

"Yeah, a red one!" piped up Sam.

Big B smiled, unsure if he wanted to commit right then to getting a surfboard back in the water. Instead, he said, "Later, guys!" and waved as everyone headed out into the bright star-filled night.

Big B picked up his backpack and his still-damp sweatshirt and then headed to his room. He sat down hard on his bed, worn out from the night's thrilling adventures.

Just as he was getting comfortable on his bed, something tapped at his window. Big B sat up and stared at the window. After a few seconds, he quietly walked over and peeked through the curtains. Tap, tap, tap. A little finger pecked at the window. Big B slid open the glass. Sam looked up at him.

"Hey, Gallo."

"What?"

"I just wanted to say thanks. Thanks for helping me and for helping the Professor."

"Hey, I'm always up for an adventure."

"Oh, and sorry."

"For what."

"Not trusting you."

"Yeah, well . . . I guess sometimes trust has to be earned."

"Yeah, and I guess sometimes it takes me a little time."

"No worries, Poni."

"See you tomorrow?"

"Yeah."

Sam darted off into the night.

Chapter 29

the trust fund

just as Big B parked himself on his bed and was settling in to think about everything that had happened and enjoying the fact that Sam was his friend again, his mother knocked on the door frame and poked her head in. "We need to talk, Brett."

Oh-oh, he thought. *That long talk.*

He knew that he and Sam and Nalu had done a good thing. They'd helped to cure his grandpa. They'd found where the toxic chemicals were flowing down into Ma'ema'e Reef. They'd gotten Sam's Stone of Souls back. And he had sacrificed his marvelous anamorphoscope in the doing of all that. The more he thought about it, the more virtuous he felt.

Right, he thought, as his mother pulled up his desk chair alongside him. *And I learned how to surf. And . . .*

"You were grounded. I trusted you to stay in your room until we got back from that endless awards dinner. Can you imagine how terrified I was when I saw that you were gone?"

"Yeah, I guess. Sorry. Yeah, that must have been a surprise."

Her voice took on a rather sharp edge, making him pay attention. "You were gone and you deliberately disobeyed me, after doing something I never dreamed you would do—breaking into your grandfather's study!"

Oh-oh. This was going to get ugly. His mother didn't raise her voice very often, and when she did it made him feel really awful. "I *said* I was sorry, Mom."

That didn't come out quite right. Her lips disappeared into a clenched line of disappointment. "I mean, I *am* sorry. I'm sorry I upset you."

That wasn't working, either; he could tell by her mouth. But how could he explain about the pirate ghosts and the putrid stream and the *Bloodlust* and make her understand? *I can't*, he thought. It suddenly became very clear to him. *I can't explain it.*

"That was a really stupid thing to do, Mom. I knew better. And I know I was grounded. I wanted to help Grandpa." For a second he thought of blaming Sam for calling him out of captivity, but he remembered her saying "I trust you." The way his mother had trusted him, and maybe now she wouldn't. *Trust can be lost*, he thought. *Like treasure.*

"That's better," she said, for some reason sounding relieved. "Now we can start over. You will leave your grandpa's things alone and you'll tell me where you're going and you'll never scare me like that again, okay?"

"Okay, Mom." He realized that she had been more afraid of his getting hurt or lost than she'd been angry about breaking the lock on the study door.

Did he dare ask if he was still grounded?

"You don't have to stay in your room. Let's just say what you did for your grandpa balances out what you did to his study. A clean slate. A new start."

She reached over, gave him a hug, and got up to leave. At the doorway she turned to look at him. "Are you all right, Brett?"

Big B's mouth curled into a smile. "Yeah, Mom. This place is palekai-ko." She almost laughed and disappeared down the hall.

Big B flopped back down on his bed, wide-eyed with relief. He was so stunned that he almost didn't recognize the sound of his cell phone, which hadn't rung since his arrival on the island. But there it was! The Bent Lizard tune that told him somebody was calling him.

Chapter 30
A Nui Start

Big B flipped open his phone. The screen read *Incoming Call.*
"No way!" Big B said in disbelief.

A face appeared, identifying the caller. For a split second, Big B thought the dark blonde receding hairline might belong to Ratbeard. Realizing with relief that it was his father's face, he pushed the talk button.

"Dad?" he said, apprehensively.

"Hey, Sport! How's it going? I've been trying to get ahold of you all weekend with no luck."

"Yeah, the reception's . . . kind of strange out here."

"Well, I understand. How's your grandpa doing?"

"Good. Actually, he's great! I think he's getting better." Big B smiled.

"That's really wonderful. Glad to hear it. Hey, I'm planning to head out there in a few weeks."

"Where are you now, Dad?"

"Shanghai. I'm interested in this new company. Yong Sheng Technologies. They manufacture tons and tons of plastic. And the strange thing is that they actually have some dealings with a company on the island. Gray Industries."

Big B remembered his grandfather's notes on the Gray Industries Annual Report. "Oh . . . um . . . that's great."

"So, Brett. I just paid for the damage to Rocco's window for you."

"Oh." Big B's heart sank. He'd forgotten about Rocco's after the night's adventure. "Thanks, Dad. Um . . . I'll, uh, pay you back . . . somehow."

"Yes, you will. You might consider doing some jobs for your grandfather this summer. A lot of jobs."

"Okay, I'll ask."

"Hey, you take care of your mom, Sport."

"I will, Dad. Good luck with your company. I'll see you in a few."

"You bet! Bye."

"Bye, Dad."

Big B clicked off his phone and flipped it closed.

He pulled the metal box out of his backpack. *If I can find the treasure, then I can pay Dad back.* He looked at the blue design painted on its porcelain lid. It reminded him of the designs on Chinese take-out boxes his dad sometimes brought home for dinner. There was one image that looked like a fruit tree. There were two symbols in the middle that were formed by its branches. The left one looked kind of like a *K* and the other one looked like another little tree. There were designs in each of the corners that looked like the cave bats, and another larger bat upside down in the middle between the two characters. At the top of the tree was another fancy-looking bird. Big B ran his fingers over the smooth surface, and opened the lid.

Inside was the compass. It appeared to be made of gold with inlaid wood and jewels. There was a fancy *W* on one side and an *S* on the other. West and south? He thought, No, that can't be right. South should be on the bottom.

"William Sneath!"

There were numbers all around the outer edge, and these were rimmed by blue stones, sapphires. Inside that circle was a spinning ring with letters. The spinning ring seemed to line up with both the numbers on its outer edge and symbols on its inner edge. In the middle was a round lid. A large pearl, perfectly set in its center, was surrounded by more blue sapphires. They reminded Big B of the eyes in his lost-forever anamorphoscope.

When he popped open the lid on the compass, he saw a round piece of glass protecting the nautical compass within. He saw *north, south, east,* and *west,* and all the directions in between. The needle swiveled delicately when he turned the compass. He closed the lid and turned the compass over. On the back there was an inscription: *Long-lived are not those who live long but those who live life fruitful.*

A noise at the door made him jump.

"Brett? Don't forget to take a quick shower tonight."

"Okay, Mom."

He quickly put the compass back inside the box and closed the lid. He pulled out the magnifying glass and his cell phone from his backpack and set them on the desk. Then he pulled out the ship's log and put it on his bed. Krill's feather slipped out of the book and floated slowly back and forth down to the ground.

"Wow, I forgot about that."

Big B picked up the feather and held it up to the light. The rainbows trapped within its soft barbs seemed almost like a holograph, appearing and disappearing depending on how he held it. Big B glanced at the ship's log. He had an idea. He opened the desk drawer and pulled out a ballpoint pen. He pried off the blue plastic cap on its end and stuffed the shaft of the feather into the opening at the pen's end. He held it up.

"Krill's quill," he said with a smile and tucked it back into the desk drawer.

He stashed the silver box and magnifying glass in the leather bag he kept underneath his bed. Then he grabbed the ship's log and slid it, along with the leather bag, back under the bed. He plugged his cell phone into its charger and headed across the hall to take a quick shower.

Big B ran the water hot. Steam and humidity began to fill the bathroom. He was surprised at how good a hot shower felt after all that had happened. As he rinsed the soap from his head, the water spilled over and pooled in his ears. He heard the funny gurgling noises that reminded him of the hot springs. The gurgles suddenly became understandable and he heard someone's voice tumbling, muttering deep inside his ear.

"Find the map!" Big B opened his eyes, letting soap slip in.

"Ow!"

He let the water run down his face and then quickly batted his eyes open and shut to flush out the soap. Closing his eyes tightly, he moved his head from side to side to wash the suds from his ears. The water tapped onto his forehead and he heard the words in his head again: "Find the map!" The water suddenly went ice cold.

Big B grabbed for the faucet, eyes still closed. He shut off the water, turning the knobs forcefully. He stood there dripping in shock. *When is this going to end?* he wondered.

Just as he stepped out of the shower onto the bath mat, he saw that a jagged line had been drawn in the steam that fogged the mirror. It looked like a tropical leaf. Drops of water formed at its points and slid down the mirror like blood.

Big B wrapped a towel around his waist and ran for the door. He burst into the hallway in a cloud of hot steamy mist and ran, slipping, toward his room.

He locked his door and stood for a moment, wet and dripping, trying to slow his speeding heartbeat. His breath slowed as he dried himself off. He could feel calm returning to his body as he dressed. He sat down on his bed and decided to take another look at the ship's log.

Reaching under the bed to locate the log, he noticed that there were things under there that hadn't been there before: three of his grandfather's journals. Two he recognized. They had brown fabric covers. One title read *Advances in Water Webs*, the other, *Advances in Conservation Reserves*. They must have been the journals from the Cruiser. *It must have been Grandpa.* He looked at the other journal. This journal was red and had no title. Inside on the first page was his name, Brett Harrington. Below that was a strange phrase, written also in his grandpa's hand in ink.

Path Find Me. Feathered It Runs.

"Path? Feathered?" he muttered. The rest of the pages were completely blank. He pulled out Krill's quill from the desk and stared at the strange riddle on the page. His mind tried to untwist the letters without any luck. He needed to work it out the way Sam had. He focused on the first phrase.

PATH FIND ME

He worked on unscrambling the words until they spelled something else. He eventually came up with

IF MAN DEPTH

He tried again, this time coming up with

FIND THE MAP.

Feeling a shiver, he knew from his experience in the shower that had to be it.

He looked at the next phrase.

FEATHERED IT RUNS.

Those words made him think of Krill.

IF RUDE THREATENS.

Hmmm. Maybe? Find the Map. If Rude Threatens. No, that can't be it. He tried again.

THE SAFE INTRUDER.

Nope. He tried again. This time he came up with

FIND THE TREASURE.

That was it! Definitely it!

He wrote it all together.

Find the Map. Find the Treasure.

He smiled. *Maybe I'm a cryptographer after all.* He turned the page and wrote his first entry.

June 2
Ending my first week in paradise
Sam and Nalu are really nice
Grandpa's back, no longer cursed
If there is a map, I'll find it first

He laughed to himself. It sounded more like a rap than some cool pirate writing. He made the beat of an air drum, and then rapped his rhyme while drawing a new tattoo on his arm with his pen. He drew a skull and crossbones, then added a crest of hair on the top, like a rooster's. He returned the quill to the desk and placed the ship's log and journals back under his bed.

Almost as soon as Big B turned off his light he fell into a deep sleep. That night he dreamed of Krill's feather. Its black rainbows illuminated his mind. Suddenly, the feather turned from black to red and then into a flame. The flame grew and grew. From out of the flame flew Krill. The bird screeched at him. Big B twisted in his sleep trying to escape his vision. But then Krill turned back into flames. Red, orange, yellow, and blue flames. He saw the rainbows once again, trapped this time in the fire. The fire then became something else. Another bird. This time it was not a seagull. It was a big, beautiful, colorful tropical bird. The bird looked at him in his dream. It was perched on a branch, surrounded by big tropical leaves shaped just like the one that had appeared in the bathroom mirror. It squawked.

"Brawk! Find the map!"

Big B awoke with a racing pulse. He sat up and rubbed his eyes, distancing himself from the vision of his dream and adjusting to the bright light of day that was filling his room. Slowly he got out of bed and stretched.

He still couldn't believe he had figured out Ratbeard's clues, recovered Sam's stone, restored Grandpa's health, and stopped the water, cutting off the pollution that was feeding the deadly red tide and the pirates. *I actually made it happen. I made a difference!* And this time, his friends stuck by him. This time, he didn't bomb.

If now he could only figure out more of Ratbeard's codes, find the map if there was one, and uncover the hidden treasures. For Big B, the challenge of these discoveries fueled a new sense of hope and excitement. Logic told him that the treasures were probably gone after all these years, but something else inside him, something he couldn't explain, made him feel like the impossible was possible. *Think big.*

He walked over and gazed out his window. His heart fluttered and he almost forgot to breathe. To his astonishment, he saw the most glorious rainbow he had ever seen shimmering over all of Vista de los Espiritus. It felt like a message of hope, just for him.

Wind chimes tinkled a cheery tune, catching the morning breeze through the opened window. Big B ran his fingers through his messy hair, styling it up into a comb of points. He smiled, feeling fresh and alive. Off in the distance somewhere he could hear a rooster crowing, announcing the new day. For Big B it wasn't just a new day. It was a new start. A Nui start.

He leaned out his window and at the top of his lungs yelled back, "Cocka-doodle-doo!"

Epilogue
Where?

t he Professor walked cautiously up through the valley and approached the springs. He scanned the area through his glasses,
and then with gloved hands. He turned over dozens of rocks,
logs, and clumps of vegetation but could not find a single bone or
clamshell.

*Strange. Hmmm. Maybe the heavy rains washed them down the valley, maybe
even into the sea*, he thought. He walked farther up the hill toward the
spot where he had seen the glowing blue light and the lightning strike.
He carried a piece of paper titled *Ma'ema'e Water Analysis*, riddled with
ominous words like *dioxin, mutagen*, and *endocrine disruptor*. The Professor
was silent as he walked. He was perplexed. The stream, the life-blood of

the valley, barely flowed; just a few trickles of water were coming into it from the sides of the valley.

He cautiously approached the spring. The water was as still as glass. A large rock was submerged halfway, sitting directly in the center of the pool, blocking the flow of water that came from within the mountain. Next to the pool was a splintered branch laid over another smaller rock, like the fulcrum of a seesaw.

"Well done, my boy." The Professor smiled proudly. He looked back at the plugged spring, shaking his head. *This water source has most definitely been tainted with some very scary chemicals. Where was the pollution coming from, and now that the spring was plugged, where was it going?* Questions about the island's water web now plagued the Professor's mind, even more than the curse of the Bone Pirates.

Little things **YOU** do have a **NUI** impact
big
important
abundant

S urfing across and diving under the curling waves of the ocean are among the most amazing adventures that we have ever experienced. Immersing into water pulsing with life in its billions of amazing forms helps put our lives in perspective. The water that surrounds us is the same water that flows through us. It is all connected. Water is life.

How we decide to treat water is how we decide to treat life itself. Water holds the memory of what has been put into it, and is the barometer of the health of our planet and its inhabitants.

When we see the faces of smiling dolphins swimming around us while we are floating in the endless blue of the sea, we can't help but smile, too. Especially since they help keep sharks away! But sometimes when I look into the eyes of a dolphin I want to say, "I'm sorry." I'm sorry that his body contains dozens of toxic chemicals. Chemicals that people let flow into their ocean home.

Pesticides sprayed onto lawns, poisons flushed down drains, trash tossed in the street, or waste dumped into rivers all flow downstream, and oceans are downstream from everyone. And those same chemicals that poison dolphins can poison us in fish we might have for dinner. It might even come back to us in the water from our taps.

Water connects everything and everyone.

As scary as pollution may feel, solutions exist and you can help. We can stop it. By taking simple steps to make your home and lifestyle healthier, you will also make the world healthier. To learn how to reduce toxins and live cleaner and greener, visit the website HealthyChild.org. To learn how to help our personal favorite sea creatures, dolphins and whales, visit our website, SurfersForCetaceans.com. Nui donates $1 from each copy of this book sold to support the nonprofits Healthy Child Healthy World and Surfers for Cetaceans. We think that's pretty cool. And remember, the next time you touch water, you touch a dolphin—and he touches you.

Peace,
Hannah Fraser & Dave Rastovich

Hannah Fraser, also known as Hannah Mermaid, travels the world to exotic locations to be filmed and photographed as a mermaid swimming in coral reefs with dolphins, whales, sea lions, and turtles, bringing attention to the magical beauty of the ocean. Her husband, Dave Rastovich, is an inspiring professional free surfer and environmentalist. They live in Byron Bay, Australia.

nui is an innovative company wholly devoted to the healthy future of youth. By creating truly healthy nutrient-rich hybrid beverages and foods to fuel growing bodies, producing exciting eco-logical adventures to expand the horizons of exploring minds, and providing opportunities to give back through charities and to network with kids worldwide, Nui supports the bodies, minds, and hearts of youth today and future generations to follow.

And little things we do have a Nui impact, too. For example, the book you have just read was printed on recycled paper with soy inks, and our publisher, Greenleaf Book Group, operates a Tree Neutral™ program to offset paper use by planting trees (www. treeneutral.com). This is certainly a choice Professor Prune would surely commend. Small choices like these can add up and make a big difference, and make a big, important, abundant—or Nui— impact on the earth. Together we can make a difference. You've already had an impact just by reading this book since Nui donates 50 percent of its profits to charities that empower youth.

Dream Big and Treasure Life.

Explore, connect, play, and take action at

About the Authors

B. T. Hope

Little things you do can have a Nui impact. When you come together
and cooperate with another, you can share the most exciting vision of
the future: **Hope.**

Brian Machovina has worked in many mission-driven organizations, fueled by his lifetime passion for the environment. As
a co-founder of Nui, he helps develop food, beverage, and
media projects that empower children to improve their physical, social,
and environmental health. He has imported and marketed community-
grown organic foods and rainforest products, co-developed a charity
that preserved rainforests and supported indigenous communities in
Latin America, and directed a coalition of organizations that protected
California waters from pollution. Prior to these activities, he was an
ecologist studying, teaching, and performing research on wetland and
marine ecology in South Florida, where he was fortunate enough to hold
in his hands everything from rattlesnakes and alligators to mysterious
amphiumas and pygmy sperm whales. He lives in Los Angeles where he
runs Nui with his high school sweetheart wife, Eileen McHale, and their
good friend David Marshall.

tina DiCicco is a designer, illustrator, and storyteller whose
work you may discover in upcoming children's books and ani-
mation, including *Ticklebug Farm, Ticklebug Zoo, Mrs. Topsy and
Mr. Turvy, Polka Dot, Applepotamus Pie,* and *Noodlehead.* A graduate in
Illustration from Rhode Island School of Design, Tina has worked as

a professional artist for seventeen years. She has designed everything from packaging and catalogs to logos and displays for active-lifestyle companies such as Nui, CamelBak Hydration Systems, Buff Multifunctional Headwear, The Yellow Rose Foundation for Type 1 Diabetes, and even the Jet Propulsion Laboratory at NASA. Tina's designs are literally out of this world (35 million miles away) on Mars. She even signed the Atlas V rocket, enhanced by her logo, before its liftoff. When she's not going into orbit for her clients or handling her responsibilities as a full-time mom, Tina builds homemade fountains, creates whimsical garden sculptures, and escapes to Nui Island, her favorite place on Earth. She resides in Sonoma County with her two monster-cats, a patient husband, and two brilliant daughters.